Keeping
the Faith

Tales from Grace Chapel Inn

Keeping the Faith

PAM HANSON &
BARBARA ANDREWS

Guideposts
New York, New York

Keeping the Faith

ISBN-10: 0-8249-4869-6
ISBN-13: 978-0-8249-4869-6

Published by Guideposts
16 East 34th Street
New York, New York 10016
www.guideposts.org

Distributed by Ideals Publications, a Guideposts company
2630 Elm Hill Pike, Suite 100
Nashville, TN 37214

Library of Congress Cataloging-in-Publication Data has been applied for.

Cover by Deborah Chabrian
Design by Marisa Jackson
Typeset by Aptara

Printed and bound in the United States of America
10 9 8 7 6 5 4 3 2 1

Acknowledgments

To our friends at West Virginia University Federal Credit Union. Thank you for your encouragement.

—Pam Hanson & Barbara Andrews

GRACE CHAPEL INN

A place where one can be
refreshed and encouraged,
a place of hope and healing,
a place where God is at home.

Chapter One

*A*lice Howard drove through sun-drenched Pennsylvania farm country, the pavement ahead a shimmering heat mirage. She had her window down, preferring the breeze of a warm August day to the artificial blasts of cold air from the air-conditioning.

She was late returning from Potterston Hospital where she'd worked the day shift. As a part-time nurse, she filled in wherever there was a need, and today she'd been on duty in the emergency room. Fortunately for the patients, it had been a day of minor injuries and easily treated illnesses. It wasn't the demands of nursing that had kept her there for an extra hour. She'd had an important meeting, and she was eager to tell her sisters about it.

She wondered whether she should have called to say she would be late, but they knew her job sometimes required overtime. No doubt Louise, a widow and her elder by three years at age sixty-five, was busy giving a piano lesson. Jane, age fifty, had no end of things to do as chef for the bed-and-breakfast they ran together in the large Victorian home their father had left them. Her sisters would be watching for her, but they wouldn't be anxious yet.

Coming home to Acorn Hill was always a pleasure. Today as she drove through town the summer sun gave the familiar one- and two-story buildings and small shops a special appearance. They stood out in sharp relief, their colors brighter and more vibrant under a cloudless azure sky.

The heat of late afternoon had driven most of the residents inside, but a pair of schoolboys was racing down the middle of Chapel Road on their bikes, prompting her to stop the car until they were safely beyond the big house ahead that was now Grace Chapel Inn. Alice didn't begrudge them their bit of wild fun. In fact, she was happy to park beside the road long enough to take in the beauty of the inn's neighbor, Grace Chapel, its steeple pointing toward heaven. The church and the faith it represented had been the focus of their family's life as long as she could remember. Her father Daniel had served as its congregation's minister and leader. He'd never ceased reaching out to his flock right up to the time of his death at age ninety-two.

Instead of hurrying inside after she drove on and parked the car, she remembered Jane's concerns about the inn's garden and decided to look for herself. They were long overdue for a good rain, and her sister was hard-pressed to keep it watered. The town council had asked residents to save water by not running sprinklers on their lawns, and Jane had cooperated, trying to keep her many flowers and the rows of vegetables alive by carrying water in the big sprinkling can. That way not a drop was wasted, but the plants had a chance to survive.

Their lawn had a few brown dry patches, but the sisters were fortunate to have long-established grass that would probably come back as soon as rains came to soak the parched ground. Some lawns in the new development on the outskirts of town weren't as fortunate. The grass there had shallow roots and was already showing signs of terminal distress. It was a hardship to the owners not to water, but for the most part, the residents had taken the possible water shortage seriously.

Jane had paid special attention to make sure the roses had enough water. Some had been planted by their parents and were a living memorial to them. The neatly spaced rows of vegetables seemed to be in good shape, the lacy carrot tops, radishes and tomato plants promising a good harvest. Unfortunately, not all the flowers were flourishing. The annuals were suffering, especially the impatiens, which were drooping for lack of a good soaking. All in all, Jane was doing her best to conserve water without letting the garden become a complete loss.

Alice went into the kitchen expecting to find her younger sister, but Jane wasn't there. She heard the somewhat labored notes of piano music coming from the parlor. Louise usually closed the door to muffle the sound of her students, but she must have left it open today for the sake of better ventilation. The lower floor of the inn stayed comfortable on the hottest days, but it did help to open doors and windows for better circulation.

Bursting with news but without anyone to tell, she went to her room on the third floor, the second-floor rooms being reserved for the inn's guests. Nothing appealed to her more at the moment than a cool shower and a change of clothes, unless it was a short catnap on her bed.

Alice loved her room. The walls were painted a buttery yellow, the perfect background for the pastel yellow, green and violet antique quilt on her bed. She kicked off her nursing shoes and wiggled her toes on the hand-braided rug, thankful that she didn't suffer from the foot problems that plagued many of her fellow nurses. How many miles did she walk every day in the hospital corridors?

The shower revived her, as expected, and she no longer felt the need for a nap. Instead she slipped into a housecoat and sat on her bed with pillows bunched behind her back, reading a professional journal that had sat on the nightstand for several weeks. She liked to be up-to-date on the latest nursing practices, but sometimes she fell behind.

An hour later, Alice was dressed in crisp white walking shorts and a pink T-shirt, her reddish brown hair, lightly streaked with gray, curling on her forehead. She felt refreshed and cooler, but she was still eager to share her news. No doubt her sisters would be meeting in the kitchen for their evening meal by now.

Louise was ushering out her last student of the day as Alice came down the stairs. Louise looked cool and unruffled even though the gangly boy with her was one of her most troublesome pupils. She'd debated refusing to give Charley more lessons, but his mother had pleaded with Louise to give him one more chance.

"How did the lesson go this time?" Alice asked when they were alone.

"A bit better, although I knew he would rather be out riding his bike."

Louise patted her short silver hair and took off the wire-rimmed glasses fastened to a chain around her neck. Her soft blue eyes, so different from her sister's dark brown ones, were lightly shadowed, a contrast to her pale skin. The nurse in Alice suspected that her sister was just plain tired today. It had been a busy week at the inn, and Louise tended to take on quite a few outside activities, especially her volunteer work at the chapel.

"I saw two boys racing their bikes down Chapel Road," Alice said. "I think one of them was Charley. Maybe his friend was still in the vicinity waiting for the lesson to be over."

"That would explain why he was so antsy to leave. At least he practiced a bit more this week. I don't know why mothers are so eager to make pianists out of children who have absolutely no interest. I think he might be better served by trying a band instrument. He seems to like being part of a group, and something loud and booming might suit him better." Louise smiled. "You can lead a horse to water, but you can't make it drink."

"Well, I have some news. Let's find Jane, and I can tell both of you at once."

Somewhat to Alice's surprise, Jane was nowhere to be seen. The kitchen, her younger sister's command base, was empty, although it showed signs that Jane had given it a thorough cleaning that day. The black-and-white checker-board floor tiles were gleaming from a fresh polishing, and the appliances sparkled without a smear to be seen. The maple butcher-block counters couldn't have looked cleaner if Jane had just sanded them down, and the curtains, white with black and red trim to match the floor and the rusty-red paint on the cupboards, looked freshly laundered and ironed. None of this was the least bit surprising. Jane kept the kitchen in immaculate condition, but it was unusual that there was no sign that she'd started dinner.

Louise and Alice were willing to take turns preparing their evening meal, but Jane much preferred to do it herself. She loved cooking, and was, in fact, a professional chef whose talents did much to attract guests to their bed-and-breakfast.

"Did she leave a note?" Louise asked. "Perhaps there's something we can do to get dinner started."

"Not that I can see. The kitchen is so sparkling clean that I'd hate to do anything to mess it up."

Louise laughed, albeit a bit wearily. "The last thing Jane would want is the two of us rummaging around in her spotless kitchen."

"That's the truth." Jane came in from the storage room carrying a bunch of newly harvested carrots. Her face was pink from being out in the sun, and her ponytail was coming undone, stray wisps of hair dangling on either side of her face. The knees of her jeans were slightly soiled, a sign that she'd been kneeling in the garden, but her sleeveless yellow-and-white striped shirt looked fresh.

Their younger sister had fair skin and vibrant blue eyes, a pleasing contrast to her dark brown hair. She was taller and thinner than either of her sisters, due in no small measure to her boundless energy. Jane was a whirlwind of activity when it came to taking care of the inn and its guests, but she still made time for a variety of activities, including her art projects and visiting the elderly shut-in members of Grace Chapel.

"I bet you thought I'd forgotten about dinner," she teased, dumping the carrots in the sink and turning on the water to wash them.

"It would be a first," Louise said. "Is there anything I can do to help?"

"Nothing at all. I thought a chef's salad would be perfect on such a warm evening. I've cut strips of ham, turkey and Swiss cheese, and sliced the boiled eggs. All I have to do is assemble it, but I thought some carrot curls would be a nice touch. The ones from our garden always taste so much better than store-bought. I didn't have time to make the dressing, but the gourmet Russian I bought in Potterston last week should do nicely."

"Alice has something to tell us," Louise said, taking it upon herself to discard the carrot tops Jane had just cut off.

"It can wait until dinner," Alice said. "Shall I set the table?"

"Please do." Jane scraped the carrots and prepared to perform magic, turning them into delicate curls to garnish the salads.

Alice watched the process with interest, not sure how her sister managed to make them so thin without breaking them.

Jane assembled the salads in big glass bowls that she kept especially for that purpose. Alice was surprised at how quickly she put them together, although she was used to her sister's kitchen wizardry.

When the salads were ready, Jane warmed a pan of cloverleaf rolls from Good Apple Bakery, the town's only retail source of fresh-baked bread and pastries. She usually did all her own baking, but all three of them also appreciated store-bought goods from their local bakeshop. Unlike many bakeries that relied on ready-prepared, frozen dough, Good Apple made everything from scratch.

Louise asked a blessing on their meal. Then Alice decided she couldn't contain her news any longer.

"I'm going to be an editor," she announced.

Her sisters looked at her blankly, waiting for her to explain what she meant.

"Let me start at the beginning," she said. "You know the hospital has been interested in having a wellness program for some time. I'm on the committee to work out the details."

"That's why you've had so many meetings after work?" Jane asked.

"Yes. The committee came to the conclusion that what's needed is better health education. They want to put out a periodic newsletter for the staff. I had a lot of doubts when they asked me to head it up, but I wholeheartedly believe in preventive medicine. Fitness is the beginning of good health, and what better place to start than with our own employees. Many of them work in high-stress situations, and medical personnel are notorious for neglecting their own health while giving their all to patients. I agreed to head up the newsletter. I do hope I'm not in over my head."

"What exactly will you have to do?" Louise asked, always the practical sister.

"Fortunately, the job of laying out the newsletter and getting it printed and distributed will be done by the hospital administration. As editor, I'll have to find people to write articles and make sure their ideas fit into the program. Other than that, I'll have to learn as I go along."

"It sounds as though it will be a lot of work," Louise said thoughtfully. "Are you sure you have time?"

"I'll make time," Alice said, remembering to take a bite of her salad. "Don't worry, I'll still be able to do my share in running our inn."

"I do not doubt that," her older sister explained. "I just don't want you to be overextended. You do so much already."

"If I can find good people to contribute, it really shouldn't be that hard. There are many at the hospital who think a wellness program is vitally important. I just have to convince them that they can reach their fellow employees through a newsletter."

"I suppose the doctors will be willing to contribute," Jane said.

"Yes, but they're the busiest people I know. I can't rely too heavily on them. I want to tap community resources beyond the hospital."

"I can see why they asked you to do it," Jane said. "You know so many people in Potterston, not to mention Acorn Hill."

"Yoo-hoo. Anyone home?" a familiar voice trilled from the front entryway.

Jane was the first to respond, hurrying out to greet their aunt.

"Goodness, I hope I'm not interrupting your supper," Ethel Buckley said. "I thought you would be done by now."

"You're not interrupting, Aunt Ethel. We're always delighted to have you drop in. We're having chef's salads. Can I fix you a plate?"

"No, thank you, dear. I had my meal an hour ago. At my age, I can't afford to eat twice."

Jane smiled at her aunt's mention of age, since Ethel's was a closely guarded secret. She was their father's younger half-sister and his only surviving sibling. When her husband Bob, a lifelong farmer, passed on, she found life in the country very lonely. Daniel Howard had persuaded her to move into the small structure that had once served as a carriage house. It had a dollhouse charm that suited her well, and its proximity to the inn allowed him to keep an eye on her without seeming to.

Ethel had taken to life in Acorn Hill with enthusiasm, making friends and indulging her lively interest in the activities of everyone around her. Sometimes Ethel was a bit flighty, but no one could doubt that she was kindhearted.

Today she looked flushed and overheated, her bright red hair a bit mussed. Her answer to the heat was a cotton sundress with white magnolias on a pale green background. It was unusual for her to wear a sleeveless garment since she was self-conscious about the heaviness of her upper arms, although she never seemed bothered by her overall plumpness.

"I have some freshly made punch," Jane said when her aunt was seated at the table and everyone had greeted her. "Can I tempt you with a glass?"

"You can indeed. That would be lovely, Jane."

The sisters finished their meal while Ethel contentedly sipped her punch, a delicious blend of tea, orange juice, lemon juice and ginger ale. Jane added the ginger ale to individual servings and garnished them with fresh mint leaves. Her aunt sighed with contentment as she sipped the refreshing drink.

"I didn't stop by so you could pamper me with this delicious beverage," Ethel said.

Jane smiled, knowing that Ethel loved to be pampered, no matter what form it took.

"What I need is to borrow your smallest stepladder."

"We have a little three-step one that I use to clean high shelves and such," Jane said, "but why do you need it?"

"Both bulbs in my living room ceiling fixture are burnt out. You made me promise never to climb up on a chair, so I thought I'd borrow the ladder to change them."

"You'll do no such thing," Jane said firmly. "I'll change them for you."

She'd lectured their aunt about taking risks that might lead to a fall, knowing that older people were especially vulnerable. Ethel agreed in principle, but she could be a little impatient when she wanted something done.

"It's a bit gloomy without ceiling light," Ethel pointed out unnecessarily.

"I'll go over and do it now."

"Oh, I don't want to interrupt your dinner," their aunt protested weakly.

"We're done," Alice assured her.

"I'll be happy to clear the table while Jane replaces your bulbs," Louise said.

"I have some that I bought in town," Ethel said. "You don't know how much I appreciate your help."

Jane started to leave with her when Alice called her back.

"You've forgotten something," she said.

Jane gave her a blank look.

"Climbing on chairs isn't any safer for you than for Aunt Ethel. Aren't you going to take the little step stool with you?"

"Yes, I should follow my own advice, shouldn't I?" Jane asked with a light laugh, as she went into the storage room to retrieve it.

Alice and Louise looked at each other and laughed too.

Jane didn't waste any time going to change her aunt's light bulbs. She carried the little step stool over to the carriage house where Ethel opened the door for her.

It was always pleasant to walk into her aunt's little nest. She'd brought favorite pieces of furniture from her farmhouse and made it into a cozy retirement home. She watched with a pleased expression while Jane set about doing the job.

"I do so appreciate how well you look after me," Ethel said. "When I was younger, I didn't realize how many little chores would become difficult in later years. My Bob always did the heaviest jobs, of course, but I mostly took care of the inside of the house, moving furniture to vacuum, climbing up to polish ceiling fixtures, cleaning the top shelves of cupboards and closets. It frustrates me that I have to ask you to do so many things for me now."

"Please don't feel that way," Jane said. "It's a pleasure having you here with us. The few things you ask of us are no trouble at all."

"You're gracious to say so, but I still never expected to be so helpless about so many things."

"You're hardly helpless," Jane said with a sympathetic chuckle. "You keep this place spotless, and your flowers look better than mine this year. Not to mention that you do so much of your own shopping and volunteer for jobs at the chapel."

She didn't add that her aunt also knew more about what went on in Acorn Hill than she and her sisters combined, due at least in part to her friendship with Florence Simpson. The two of them loved to keep their fingers on the pulse of everything that happened in town. It certainly kept Ethel entertained, even though she was prone to gossip.

"Speaking of shopping," Ethel said as she watched Jane climb up to remove the frosted-glass light globe, "I'm afraid. I'm going to have to buy a few summer things. I wonder if they've had the end-of-the-season sales in Potterston yet."

"I imagine Florence would know more about that than I do, but I think you have quite a nice wardrobe of summer clothing."

"I do, but I'm having a bit of a problem. I think the dry cleaners shrunk my best suit, and several of my dresses seem a tad tight. Maybe I'm washing them in water that's too warm."

Jane climbed down with the globe and walked to the kitchen sink to wash it out before replacing it. She surely didn't want to point out that it was unlikely her aunt's clothes were tight because they'd shrunk.

"Of course, I know I've gained a few pounds," Ethel went on. "Florence and I were talking about it just yesterday. It's so hard to keep one's girlish figure, you know. Still, you're so active all the time that you probably never give it a thought."

Jane knew how sensitive her aunt was. She wouldn't dream of commenting on her weight. It was a subject best avoided altogether, so she didn't respond to Ethel's weight talk.

"I'll put the bulbs in. Then you can hand me the globe," she said instead.

"I bought this funny new kind," Ethel said removing two cardboard-encased bulbs from a plastic sack. "They're supposed to save energy and last a long, long time. I thought that sounded good, even though they were quite expensive compared to the regular ones."

Jane reached up to screw in the first of the fluorescent bulbs. Although it looked larger in her hand because of the odd shape of the circular glass tubes, she found that it fitted in the space quite nicely. Ethel handed her the second one, then the globe.

Together they stood below it and looked up.

"I was afraid it might be dimmer," Ethel said, "but it really has a nice glow, doesn't it?"

"Yes, I don't think you'll notice any difference in the amount of light. It was a good idea to invest in the energy-saving bulbs."

Ethel glowed, too, always appreciating praise from her nieces.

"Maybe I'll just purchase a few things from one of my mail-order catalogs," she said, jumping back to the topic that most concerned her. "Do you think they'll still have anything lightweight?"

"I should think so. After all, there are so many people who live in warmer climates than this. But are you sure you need new clothes? Maybe it's only a temporary problem."

"I suppose I could watch what I eat for a while and see how it goes. I do have quite a few summer dresses. I don't really want to start building a new wardrobe. I love pretty clothes, but it would be so expensive to buy all new things in a larger size."

Jane didn't want to talk about clothing or size anymore for fear of hurting her aunt's feelings, but Ethel wasn't ready to let go of the subject.

"Would you take a look at my lime-green linen suit? It's my favorite outfit for church and social activities. Maybe the skirt could be let out just a bit."

"Yes, but—"

Ethel didn't wait to hear Jane's objection. She scurried into her bedroom and called out that she'd be just a minute. True to her word, she quickly returned, dressed in her pretty summer suit.

"See, it's just a trifle snug around the waist," she said, twirling around so Jane could see.

Jane's heart sank. The skirt hugged her aunt's hips in a most unbecoming way. Even if the seams were large enough to let out, the alteration would be sure to show on the light fabric. Anything she could do to make it bigger after years of wear would probably be a disaster.

"You're not saying anything," Ethel chided. "I know, you're trying to be kind by not telling me how awful it looks."

"You have had that suit for quite a few years, haven't you?" Jane guessed, judging by the style.

"That's true. Maybe I should donate it to the thrift store in Potterston. I do tend to keep my clothes too long, especially when they're favorites."

"You have some very pretty print dresses," Jane reminded her. "I don't think you'll miss one suit."

"Well . . ." Ethel now sounded reluctant to part with it. "Maybe I'll hold on to it, just in case. Would you like to see how my lavender print looks? I think the skirt is full enough to cover a few extra pounds."

Jane could see where this was going. Reluctant as she was to pass judgment on any part of her aunt's wardrobe, she didn't want to let her down by refusing.

Several clothing changes later it was clear that Ethel's wardrobe was in trouble. There were full-skirted dresses that still looked quite nice, but nearly half of her favorite outfits were on the tight side.

"I can't tell you how upset I am," Ethel said. "I really must do something about my weight."

"Why don't you talk to Alice? She's on a wellness committee at the hospital. I bet she'll have some really good suggestions for you."

"Yes, I'll do that. Thank you for looking at my outfits and listening. You've been a big help, and not just in changing the bulbs."

Jane walked back to the inn, feeling guilty for suggesting that Alice could solve their aunt's problem. She knew perfectly well why her aunt had gained weight. She lived a fairly sedentary life, and she did enjoy good food. Much of her social life revolved around luncheons with friends like Florence, and she always enjoyed being part of dinner parties at the inn. This didn't mean that her aunt overindulged. Far from it. She just didn't burn calories the way she had as a farm wife with a multitude of responsibilities that kept her on the move.

The kitchen was empty when Jane got back, but Louise and Alice had cleaned up for her and loaded the dishwasher. It was just as well that she didn't reveal their aunt's concern about her weight gain. Alice had her schedule full planning a newsletter for the hospital's wellness project. Perhaps Ethel would forget about it by tomorrow, although it was unlikely if her wardrobe was a constant reminder.

Jane made herself a cup of herbal tea and sat at the kitchen table for a long time, first thinking about her aunt, then planning the breakfast she would prepare for guests in the morning. She was fortunate. Unlike some chefs who enjoyed their own cooking too much, her main pleasure came in preparing appealing and nourishing dishes for others. She was usually satisfied with moderate portions of the food she served. Also, the demands of running the bed-and-breakfast burned far more calories than Ethel's quieter lifestyle.

She rinsed her cup, checked that the doors were locked for the night and turned off all but the night-lights. Tomorrow was another day, and it would begin early.

Chapter Two

*A*re you expecting anyone to register this morning?" Louise asked Tuesday morning as she finished a breakfast of poached eggs and smoked salmon.

Jane was enjoying her company and having a cup of orange-spice tea with her sister. All the guests had eaten and then checked out rather early, which gave her a little leisure time to visit with Louise.

"We do have one new couple coming from New Jersey, but they didn't mention what time they'll get here. They reserved a room through the thirteenth, so I hope they don't change their minds."

"Let's see, today is only the fifth. That is a long stay. Maybe they have relatives in Acorn Hill."

"Not that the wife mentioned when she called for the reservation. But you're right, it is quite an extended booking. It will be very inconvenient if they back out. We've had several cancellations in the last month, but I'm not sure why. Maybe the increasing price of gasoline has made people change their minds about vacationing."

"I imagine it's just coincidence, family emergencies and such. We've been fortunate that most of our guests are reliable," Louise said, delicately wiping her mouth on a napkin and pushing her chair away from the kitchen table. "What I should have asked is whether you need me to watch the inn this morning."

"Not if you have something else to do."

"Nothing urgent, but I need to go over to the chapel for some practice time on the organ this week. Rev. Thompson wants the congregation to learn a new song that isn't in the hymnal. It's one he learned at a retreat last month."

"That sounds interesting. He certainly knows how to keep the services fresh and inspiring. By all means, spend as much time as you like practicing. I don't have any errands that need doing immediately."

"I can help you clear the dining room table first," Louise offered.

"Thanks, but I'll take care of it. I know you like to practice in the morning when you're most alert."

"Afterward I'll drop in on Mrs. Arthur. She hasn't come to church for several weeks, and I worry about her."

"It's not because she doesn't have someone to bring her," Jane said with a worried frown. "Her neighbor is very good that way."

"The last time I saw her she was looking terribly thin. She said that food doesn't taste good to her anymore."

"Alice said that Father's appetite wasn't good toward the end. Mrs. Arthur must be ninety-four, maybe ninety-five. Shall I make up a plate of cookies to tempt her?"

"Maybe just a few of your plain sugar cookies, Jane. They're usually popular with the elderly. Don't rush to do it now, though. I'll come back for them before I go to her house."

"I'll just get them out of the freezer to thaw. Imagine, living alone at her age. You have to admire her spunk."

"I think her family would feel better if she moved to Ohio, where they could look after her. She has a daughter and several nieces who have offered to look after her." Louise smiled at her younger sister. "For my part, I feel so blessed to have you and Alice—not to mention Cynthia."

"I'm sure your daughter would object strenuously if you wanted to live alone at that age," Jane said with an indulgent smile as Louise was leaving.

Much as Jane enjoyed her sisters' company, she needed time alone early in the day to keep on top of all the jobs around the inn, not the least of which was planning meals a few days ahead. It helped immensely if guests came when they said they would. If she planned breakfast for a full house, and two people canceled at the last minute, it threw off her menu.

$\backsim$

It was late morning when the couple from New Jersey arrived. Jane was curious about their plans, but she also was too tactful to ask leading questions. Most of their visitors talked about their reasons for visiting Acorn Hill sooner or later.

"We have a reservation for a room with a private bath," the man said. "Vern and Isabel Snyper."

He was a mild-looking man with thinning gray-brown hair and a rather long nose that didn't quite fit his round face and apple cheeks. He was wearing wire-framed bifocals that rested low on his nose, and he looked at Jane over the top of them. His blue-striped sports shirt hung out over rather baggy tan pants in his botched attempt to look casual. Jane's intuition told her that he was more comfortable in a business suit and tie.

"Yes, I have your reservation here," she said. "Welcome to Grace Chapel Inn."

"That's an unusual name for a bed-and-breakfast," his wife said, a comment Jane frequently heard.

"Our father was the minister at Grace Chapel for many years," she explained. "You may have noticed it just down the road. When we inherited the house from him, it was too big to maintain as a residence, so we converted it to accommodate guests. The name honors him and our family's connection to the chapel."

"Do you welcome guests from other faiths and secular visitors as well?" Mrs. Snyper asked.

"Yes, of course." Jane was taken aback. That was a question that she had never been asked before.

Mrs. Snyper might once have been very attractive. She was slender and nearly the same height as her husband, but her face had the premature wrinkling of a sun lover. She'd been wise to leave her hair a natural salt-and-pepper instead of trying to dye it to a more youthful shade. It was styled in a sleek cap that emphasized her almond-shaped hazel eyes. Unlike her husband, she hadn't made any attempt to wear casual vacation clothes, suggesting to Jane that she was a career woman accustomed to dressing well every day. Her peacock-green dress was the latest style with an empire waist jacket embellished with embroidery work in the same shade. She further emphasized her height with spike heels in silvery snakeskin.

When the paperwork was complete, Jane located their key and invited them to follow her upstairs to their room.

"May I help with your bags?" she asked.

"Don't you have a handyman for that sort of thing?" the man asked, hefting two heavy bags himself and leaving only a makeup case for his wife to carry.

"Now, Vern, you know this is only a small operation. It hardly warrants a full-time custodian," his wife gently rebuked him.

"How many guest rooms do you have?" he asked conversationally.

"Four," Jane said. "They're all on the second level. My two sisters and I have rooms on the third floor."

"Do the guest rooms all have private baths?" his wife asked as she followed Jane up the stairs.

"No, only two do, Mrs. Snyper. The other two share a bath."

"Oh, please call me Isabel. And my husband is Vern. I'm sure we'll get to know each other well while we're here."

"I understand breakfast comes with the room," her husband said. "Do you offer lunch and dinner service for those who are willing to pay extra?"

"We do offer lunch and dinner for an additional fee, but we encourage our guests to enjoy what Acorn Hill has to offer. The Coffee Shop is nearby, and they serve a full menu. If you like a light snack, there's the Good Apple Bakery. Quite often our guests drive to Potterston where there are a number of very good restaurants."

"Do you allow cooking in the rooms?" Isabel asked.

"I'm afraid not. The fire code regulations are quite strict. There's absolutely no smoking anywhere in the inn either."

"I'm sure we'll get by," her husband said. "Neither of us smokes, and we're not the least bit fussy about what we eat."

"You don't have an elevator tucked away somewhere, maybe to haul up freight?" Isabel asked as they slowly climbed the stairs.

"No, I'm sorry. We've never felt a need for one."

"I imagine you couldn't accommodate a handicapped person even if you had one. Not without building a ramp to give access to the front porch. It must get terribly complicated to think of everything that has to be done to make a home into an inn. Quite costly too."

"We enjoy sharing our home," Jane said, "but we know we can't compete with a modern motel or hotel. We have to refer people with special needs to accommodations in Potterston. Our guests tend to be traveling business people, relatives of Acorn Hill residents and people just passing through on vacation. Do you have family here?"

"Oh no, nothing like that," Isabel said, although she didn't volunteer why they had come.

"Your room is the Garden Room. We named it that because it looks down on our garden, although I'm afraid it isn't quite as green this month as it usually is. We haven't had a good rain for some time."

"You name your rooms?" Vern asked, sounding surprised.

"We're too small to need room numbers, so that seemed a pleasant alternative. Here we are."

She opened the door and stood aside to let them enter. Most guests were immediately charmed by the lovely gardenlike decor and the beautiful rosewood bedroom set, but Vern looked around without comment.

"It's quite lovely," his wife said. "I don't want to be a bother, but would you mind terribly showing us the other rooms? I'm always fascinated by Victorian houses."

"No other guests have arrived yet, so I can let you look at them. I'll have to go down for the keys."

"I would really appreciate it," Isabel said.

Jane was more puzzled than put out as she hurried down to retrieve the other three keys. Was the new guest displeased with the room she'd reserved for her, or was she just curious? Jane was used to the oddities of guests, but this was a new request.

The Snypers were exploring the room, opening drawers and inspecting the bathroom when she returned. Their luggage was sitting near the door.

"Right across the hall is the Sunset Room," she said leading them to that door. "This room and yours are at the front of the house, but I'm sure you won't be bothered by noise from the street. Acorn Hill is a very quiet town."

The couple circled the room, taking in the terra-cotta walls and the creamy antiqued furniture. Isabel paused before each of the Impressionist prints on the walls but didn't comment. They didn't ask for a room change, and Jane invited them to see the other two.

She showed them the Sunrise Room with its large, newly restored landscape painting, and again Isabel intensely studied the art on the wall. Was the new guest a fellow art lover?

"Are you an artist or a collector?" Jane asked.

"Oh no. I do work as an interior decorator, but I seem to spend most of my time making and hanging curtains. Whoever did your rooms has a flair for design."

"It was pretty much a family project," Jane said modestly, not wanting to claim credit for what had been mostly her work.

Jane didn't follow Vern when he went to inspect the shared bathroom, but she heard him turning the faucet on and off, apparently testing rather than using it.

"The plumbing works fine," he said when he came out.

"If you'd like to see the other room," Jane said tentatively, not quite sure what to make of these new guests. They certainly were curious about the inn.

"Do you have trouble filling these back rooms without a private bath?" he asked as she showed him the last room, the Symphony Room.

"No, it hasn't been a problem," she assured him, although she had no idea why he wanted to know.

"I think the Rose Room would be a good name for this one," Isabel said, staring at the wallpaper with its pretty climbing-rose pattern.

"Tell me," Vern said, "do you have any policy about guests using the rooms downstairs?"

"We don't have any restrictions as such," Jane said, "although we do prefer that no one comes into the kitchen."

"Understandable that you'd need a private space," he said.

"Our guests particularly enjoy the front porch on warm summer evenings, but you're free to use the parlor except when my sister is giving piano lessons. And, of course, breakfast is served in the dining room, generally between seven and nine. You can let me know what time you prefer."

"I think you can put us down for eight o'clock unless something special comes up," Vern said.

Was the couple testing her in some way? Jane didn't have a clue. Certainly she wanted all their guests to feel at home, but she'd never had anyone be so inquisitive.

"Oh, piano lessons," Isabel said, sounding a bit alarmed. "Will we hear them?"

"Unlikely," Jane said. "My sister closes the door when guests are in the inn, and the parlor has been made sound-proof."

"This is a bit new to us, staying in a bed-and-breakfast," Isabel said, as though offering an excuse for checking on so many details. "I'm sure we'll enjoy our stay immensely."

Her husband agreed, but he had another question.

"Do we have the option of breakfast in our room?" he asked.

"We don't have enough help for that," she said. "But if someone was ill, we could make an exception."

"We're certainly not sick," his wife quickly said, then paused. "I am curious about the towels. Are we limited as to how many we can use in a day?"

"We've never had a need to do that. If you need more, just ask me or one of my sisters."

Were they going to be unhappy guests who complained about everything? Jane wondered. They'd had a few malcontents in the past, but it was rare that their visitors didn't appreciate all that the inn had to offer. She remembered how long the Snypers planned to stay and sincerely hoped that it would be a pleasant visit for them.

She ushered them back to their room, relieved that at least they hadn't asked for a different one. It wouldn't have inconvenienced her to switch them, but it would have boded

ill for their stay. Still, she had to admit that they were courteous and agreeable, seemingly a very nice couple. She could
understand that they might have questions if they were used
to staying in hotels and motels.

A short time later Jane heard the front door open and
close. When she went to see if other guests had arrived, she
found that the Snypers had left. They were just getting into
a black Ford parked in front of the inn.

Jane smiled at her own curiosity about these new guests.
She was as eager to know more about them as they had been
to see more of the inn.

Louise felt uplifted by her long practice session. The church
had been empty and quiet, altogether the best conditions
for learning new music. She always enjoyed talking to their
minister, but he was not at Grace Chapel. Most likely he was
visiting members of the congregation at Potterston Hospital
or in senior facilities throughout the county.

Afterward she went downstairs to the kitchen. It was
her month to help care for the facility, and she was glad
to see that it was as spick-and-span as it had been after
the committee cleaned it the previous week. The chapel's
members took pride in keeping their building in good
order. Not even Florence Simpson's critical eye would find

any fault with the kitchen as it was today. Louise gathered a dishcloth and a couple of hand towels to launder, then headed home.

"Did you have a good practice?" Jane asked when she entered the kitchen.

"Excellent," Louise said. "I feel ready for Sunday service, and it's only Tuesday. Did the new guests arrive?"

"Yes, the couple from New Jersey, but they've gone out."

She gave her sister a searching look. Something in her voice told Louise that Jane was uneasy about them.

"Do they seem nice?"

"Oh yes, the woman was quite charming."

"But?" Louise quizzed her.

"Well, they did seem awfully curious. For a few moments, I felt as though they might be some kind of inspectors."

"What do you mean?"

"Well, they wanted to see all the guest rooms. I felt that they were studying them, although for what purpose I can't begin to guess. They didn't ask for a room change. The husband Vern even tested the faucets in the back bathroom. Don't you think that's a curious thing to do?"

"A bit, but then, we have had our share of eccentric guests. Most of the time they work out just fine."

"You're right, of course," Jane said. "Are you ready for lunch? I had a yen for a sliced tomato and Muenster cheese sandwich on rye, but I can fix you something else if you like."

"That's fine, but I'll just have one slice of bread. You spoil us, you know. There's always a new tasty treat with you in charge of the kitchen. Left on our own, Alice and I would live on tuna salad and TV dinners."

"I doubt that, but I'm glad you're home for lunch. Do you have plans for the rest of the day?"

"You know, since the new recycling plant opened on the edge of town, I've thought maybe it was past time to tackle some of the clutter in the attic. It's one place that we've neglected of late."

"Do you think you'll find anything to recycle up there?" Jane asked.

"Maybe not, but it wouldn't hurt to organize it a bit."

"It will be awfully hot. Are you sure you want to do it today?"

"I'll take up the portable fan. Anyway, I won't do much this afternoon, just look over the situation. One of my pupils canceled because her family is on vacation, and another is spending a week with her grandmother. It's unusual that I have a weekday afternoon with no lessons. In fact, I'm caught up with all my obligations. Of course, if you have something you need me to do—"

"Nothing at all. Just promise me that you won't stay there long if you get hot."

"I guarantee it."

After lunch Louise hauled the large square electric fan up to the attic. She had just a twinge of conscience for not telling Jane the whole truth. It was unlikely that their attic contained much of value for the recycling effort, but she needed to go through personal papers and mementos that she'd stored there years before.

When she moved back to their family home after the death of her father, her grief had still been too fresh to sort through many of the things from the life she'd shared with her husband Eliot. He had passed on four years before her father after a painful struggle with cancer. Although he'd once been her music theory teacher and was fifteen years her senior, she'd never expected to lose him so soon. When she closed their house in Philadelphia, she hadn't had the heart to go through all their possessions. Instead she'd shipped many items to Acorn Hill, and a lot of them still reposed in the attic.

She didn't suppose that she could make much headway in the hot, stuffy attic, but maybe she could carry down some things to sort in more comfortable surroundings. With that in mind, Louise tackled the first of many corrugated cardboard boxes that held parts of her past.

Jane had been right about the heat, but with the fan blowing directly on her, she soon became engrossed in the contents of a box of sheet music, some hers and some Eliot's. It was definitely time to decide what she wanted to keep. The rest could be donated to a thrift shop, especially some really old popular songs with colorful art on the covers. She was pretty sure there were collectors who would enjoy them, especially since some had been Eliot's mother's.

The old music reminded her of a bygone time when families gathered around a piano instead of a TV. The sentimental side of her was reluctant to part with them, but she knew the attic was a poor place to store anything made of paper. She'd been fortunate so far in not having pests ruin the old music. She was busy making a pile of giveaways when a voice behind her startled her into bolting upright.

"What—"

Louise stood quickly and turned.

"I'm sorry I scared you," a man said. "I tried to make noise coming up the steps so you wouldn't be alarmed."

"And you are?"

"Vern Snyper. My wife and I checked into the inn this morning."

"What on earth brings you up here?" She was much too shaken to temper her reaction.

"I've always had a fondness for old houses, ones from the Victorian era. I heard you going up the stairs to the third floor. I wanted to ask if I could see the rooms on that level, but when I realized you'd gone up to the attic, I followed you here."

She was still rattled, but not so much that she didn't remember that she'd been in the attic for several minutes.

"How long have you been standing there?"

"Oh, awhile. I guess you didn't hear me because the fan is pretty loud. I'm terribly sorry. You were so engrossed in what you were doing that I didn't know how to let you know I was here. I guess 'Hello' wasn't the best way."

Guest or not, this man deserves a scolding, Louise thought. Still, her usually courteous nature prevailed.

"There's really nothing here to see. I'm afraid we've been a bit remiss in cleaning it out," she said.

"That's only human nature. It looks like you've installed a fair amount of insulation," he said as he looked around. "My wife probably wouldn't think of doing that if the inn were hers."

"My father knew the value of it to conserve heat," Louise said a bit stiffly.

"Has it been rewired recently?"

"I assure you that it's in good condition, and we've passed all codes. We have fire and carbon-monoxide detectors on every floor. You don't need to worry about fire in the inn. We've taken every precaution to see that our guests are safe."

"Oh, forgive me again. I wasn't implying that the building is unsafe. I'm just an amateur enthusiast when it comes to old homes. In fact, my wife and I restored a Federal house built around 1810. It was a labor of love."

"That's very nice, but—"

"I know, it's still rude of me to creep about and upset you. I do hope you'll accept my apology."

Louise took a deep breath, then nodded.

"What do you know about the history of the house? Were your ancestors the original owners? I expect it was built around the 1880s or '90s. I like that you've painted the exterior in historically correct colors—cocoa siding, eggplant purple roofline trim, green shutters, white window trim. You'd be surprised how many people think gray is the way to go."

"If you'll excuse me," Louise said, in no mood to chat about the house. "It really is too hot up here today."

"Can I carry the fan down for you?"

"No, I'll just leave it here."

"I like that a man can stand upright in your attic. Ours is too cramped for comfort," Vern said. "Is there anything else I can carry for you?"

"No, no thank you."

Louise didn't know how to handle the inquisitive guest. Jane had hinted that his curiosity made her uneasy, but they'd never had a visitor so determined to explore every inch of the inn. She turned off the fan and removed the plug from the socket, hoping Mr. Snyper would take it as a signal to leave.

He didn't.

"It must be a tremendous expense to put a new roof on a home this size," he speculated.

"Yes it was."

"How often do you have to paint?"

"It depends on how well it weathers."

She made a motion to skirt around him to the exit, and finally he started to leave.

"Be careful on the steps," he warned. "A person could take a nasty fall."

Alarm bells went off in her head. She'd heard of people who faked falls in order to sue the owners of the property. The inn was well insured, of course, but this guest was making her exceedingly uncomfortable.

Much to her relief, he carefully negotiated the stairs, looking back to see that she made it safely to the third floor.

"Do you ever have guests in the rooms on this floor?" he asked casually.

"No, this is our personal living space."

"Ah yes, it would be. The two of you run the inn together? I don't think I got your name."

"Mrs. Smith. And three of us manage the inn."

"Three sisters?"

She nodded.

"Well, you seem to be doing a wonderful job, Mrs. Smith." He was flushed from the heat in the attic, but his comment sounded sincere, even though Louise was not in the mood for it.

Her instinct was to bolt into her room, but instead she waited until he went down to the second floor and disappeared into his.

How extraordinary, Louise thought. It was rare that a guest went up to the third floor, let alone to the attic.

$\backsim$

"I'd love to see an article in your newsletter about keeping feet healthy," Dorothea, the hospital's resident physical therapist said. "Too many women teeter around on ridiculously high heels when they're young, then pay the price later with bunions and arthritis—though sometimes both are more the fault of genes than behavior."

"That would be a great topic," Alice agreed. "Hospital personnel are on their feet so much. Can I count on you to write a short article, maybe five hundred to seven hundred words maximum?"

"Oh, Alice, I'd love to help you out, but I'm a terrible writer. I can't even think of anything to put on my Christmas cards. Could you possibly just interview me? I'm a much better talker than writer."

"I'll see what I can do," Alice said, trying to conceal her disappointment. "For the first issue I really need completed articles."

Her shift was over for the day, but she didn't feel free to go home yet. She'd talked to people on her break and during lunch hour, but she'd yet to find even one person who was willing to write an article. On the good side, everyone had had a positive reaction and suggested possible topics. Even Dr. Holmes, a cardiologist who had a reputation for being taciturn, was enthusiastic about reaching out to hospital staff through a newsletter. But like all the others she'd asked, he didn't see writing as his forte. Everyone was willing to talk about a subject, but no one acknowledged having the time or talent to put together an article.

It was obvious to Alice that she was going to have to do more than just edit the new publication. But how could she possibly be responsible for writing enough articles herself? Although she might enjoy talking to people, she didn't know any techniques for interviewing. As far as writing anything, she would rather work double shifts than try to make words come alive on a page. She was no journalist.

Was the newsletter doomed before it even got started? There were more people on her list of potential contributors, but she was discouraged by all the professed non-writers that she'd approached so far. Surely everyone on the staff had written term papers in their school days. What was it about putting words on paper that intimidated them?

The evening shift was just settling into work, so this wasn't the best time to approach anyone else. Alice didn't think anything more could be done that day, so she reluctantly collected her purse and keys from her staff locker and headed toward the parking lot.

She was so lost in thought that she barely noticed that someone had fallen into step beside her.

"Did you have any luck getting articles, Miss Howard?"

She looked over to see Jody Monroe, one of the younger nurses and a volunteer on the wellness committee. She was short and slightly plump with a mass of curly blonde hair framing her pretty, round face. Alice didn't know her well. They hadn't worked in the same department, and Jody was a little shy, not usually speaking up at meetings.

"Do call me Alice," she said with an encouraging smile. "And no, I'm afraid I struck out with everyone I asked."

"Oh, I'm surprised," she said, sounding genuinely disappointed. "Doesn't anyone have a good idea for an article?"

"Yes, everyone does," Alice said, slowing her pace to explain her problem. "The trouble is, no one is willing or able to work up an actual article. I found people to be interviewed, but no one to write."

"Oh, that's no problem," Jody said cheerfully.

"What do you mean?" Alice stopped a few spaces from her car and looked at the young woman with surprise.

"I'll be glad to help with that part. I am on the wellness committee, and so far no one has given me a job."

"Do you mean you'd be willing to write an article?" Much as Alice appreciated the offer, she didn't know what the novice nurse might have to offer in the way of expertise.

"Not one of my own." Her face was flushed, whether from excitement or the heat Alice didn't know.

"Oh." Alice tried not to sound disappointed.

"Before I decided to become a nurse, I was enrolled in college as a journalism student. I guess because my mom is a nursing-home supervisor, I wanted to try a different career. But I worked on the student newspaper long enough to know that I was a very bad reporter."

"You didn't like writing stories?"

"I loved it, but interviewing people was agony. I soon learned that I'm not nearly as aggressive as a good reporter needs to be. When I had an appointment to talk to someone, even a professor who would probably be friendly and helpful, I couldn't sleep the night before. It was like having my tonsils out, only worse."

"That's a shame." Alice sympathized with her but didn't know how a journalism dropout could be helpful.

"No, it was good that I learned early on what wasn't right for me. I love nursing, and it's where I belong. But if you need someone to help in writing articles, I'd be more than glad to do it."

Alice was thoughtful for a moment, thinking of ways to take Jody up on her offer.

"I wouldn't mind going along on interviews, just as long as I don't have to ask the questions. I always freeze up when it comes to getting information from people. You could tape interviews, then give them to me. I have a computer at home, so I could check facts and add additional information where it's needed. It would be fun to put some of my journalism education to work for a good cause."

"You'd be willing to use your free time to come along on interviews, then be responsible for finished articles?"

Alice had never, ever, thought of herself as a reporter, but she did like to talk to people. Teamwork just might be the answer to her problem.

"No problem," Jody said with a smile. "Truth to tell, I don't do much besides go to work. I grew up in Potterston, but most of my friends have moved away or are busy with babies and such. Mom and I are home alone most evenings because Dad works for the railroad and travels a lot."

"You've really relieved my mind. I think we can do a great newsletter working as partners." Alice grasped Jody's hand and smiled warmly. "You'll be my associate editor, and I'll see that you get full credit for your work."

"You'll let me know when you need me?"

"You can be sure of it."

Alice smiled to herself. Not only would Jody's participation be an immense help, it might build the young woman's self-esteem and help her get beyond her shyness. Alice breathed a sigh of relief, pleased by the younger nurse's offer and happy to get to know her better.

Chapter Three

*J*ane had a full house Wednesday with double occupancy in every room, a total of eight guests who'd requested breakfast at varying times from seven to eight. She turned to an old favorite, Eggs Benedict, for an elegant entrée that could be prepared individually as needed. She topped the English muffins, Canadian bacon and poached eggs with her homemade Hollandaise sauce. Instead of making it in a blender as some chefs did, today she prepared hers in the top of a double boiler, a relic that had been in the house since she was a child. She used a whisk to incorporate the egg yolks, water, butter and lemon juice, then let the warm water in the bottom part of the boiler keep it at the right temperature for serving.

Breakfast started with fresh fruit cups containing the best that was available in season, including cantaloupe, honeydew melon and peaches. A tray of honey buns was available for those with a sweet tooth.

Alice, of course, had to leave for work before the first guest came down, but Louise was on hand to keep the coffee carafe on the sideboard filled, and to clear places when guests left. She also checked out the early departures, leaving Jane free to prepare individual portions.

At last there were only two people left in the dining room, Isabel and Vern Snyper. For Jane, the hardest part of the breakfast routine was the occasional waiting to clear the table when guests lingered uncommonly long after eating. It was their prerogative, of course, and she was glad to have them enjoy their coffee in leisure. This morning, though, it seemed the couple would never leave.

"I'll fix your breakfast," Jane said to Louise. "Then you can get on with what you have planned for today. There's enough sauce left for one more serving of Eggs Benedict."

"You should have it yourself," Louise said. "You know that I'm happy with a bowl of cereal."

"I had a continental breakfast," Jane said with a smile. "I wanted to eat light."

"A hard roll and jam? That doesn't sound terribly substantial," Louise teased, watching as Jane set about fixing breakfast for her.

Louise had just begun to eat when Isabel Snyper poked her head into the kitchen.

"Good morning," she said. "My compliments to the chef. That was a lovely breakfast. I haven't had Eggs Benedict in ages, and your sauce was magnificent."

"Thank you, but it's not as difficult to make as some people believe," Jane said modestly. "I'm glad you enjoyed it."

"What a splendid kitchen," Isabel said, coming all the way into the room and looking around. "I would never have thought of doing one in black, white and red. I did expect it to be larger, though. What do you do about food storage?"

"We have a separate room," Jane said pointing toward it.

"You must have to go to the market frequently," their guest said.

"One trip a week to Potterston is usually enough. We buy what we can in town. We like to support local businesses."

"How far ahead do you plan your menu? It must be quite a chore to keep it from getting boring."

"Not at all," Jane said, beginning to feel a bit defensive. "I love cooking, and stocking up on supplies is an important part of it."

"Of course, it is," Isabel quickly said. "I'm certainly looking forward to more of your delicious breakfasts, and that's from someone who is usually satisfied with toast and coffee. If you don't mind my asking, do you get a discount from the grocers since you're a volume buyer?"

"We've never asked for one," Louise said, puzzled by the woman's interest.

"In the planning stage, do you allocate a certain dollar amount per meal, the way we used to do in home economics at school? I've always wondered how that worked in a commercial operation."

Is she worried about getting her money's worth? Jane wondered.

"We're more concerned with preparing the kind of breakfasts that will please our guests. I plan differently when families with children are here, and sometimes we serve heartier food that appeals more to men."

"I imagine costwise it averages out," Isabel said thoughtfully. "Oh, please don't think I'm suggesting that you scrimped in any way on today's breakfast. It was elegant, better than we expected."

"Thank you," Jane said, although she wasn't sure what the Snypers had expected. A bed-and-breakfast that didn't live up to the implied promise of a pleasing meal to begin the day wouldn't get many return guests.

"Well, I don't want to keep you from your work," Isabel said cheerfully, "but I do so admire what you've done with this house. It can't have been easy turning your family home into an inn. How long did it take you to do all the necessary renovations?"

"It mostly involved redecorating and getting all the licenses and permissions," Jane said, not sure she could put a time assessment on what was essentially a labor of love.

"When Vern and I renovated our little Federal period home, it was in sad shape, I can tell you. The former tenants had turned it into a shambles. We virtually stripped it down to bare boards and replaced everything—plumbing, heating, wiring, roof, you name it."

"It sounds like a huge project," Jane said.

"Fortunately, Vern is pretty handy around the house, not that he has a lot of time. He works for an investment firm and has to be on top of the market all the time. I did most of the decorating, since that's my field, but it involved a lot of research to make it authentic."

"I can imagine," Louise said, standing to take her plate and utensils to the sink. "Well, I'd best be off. I hope you enjoy your stay in Acorn Hill, Mrs. Snyper."

"Please, call me Isabel. I'm afraid I don't remember your first name."

"Louise."

"Oh, do you have a nickname? My husband calls me Izzy sometimes, but I can't say that I encourage it."

"Most people call me Louise. Have a nice day."

Jane expected the guest to follow her sister's lead, but instead she circled the kitchen, seemingly studying the cupboards and appliances.

"You certainly keep a spanking-clean kitchen. Do you have a service that comes in regularly?"

"No, I prefer to do it myself." Jane didn't know whether to go about her business or invite Isabel to sit down. "What do you have planned for your day?"

"Oh, we're on vacation, so we're not making many plans. It feels good just to follow our instincts. You might say we're here for rest and relaxation."

"Acorn Hill is a good place for that."

"Maybe we'll take a stroll around town, meet some of the shop people."

"I'm sure they'd be happy to meet you."

This is beginning to feel weird, Jane thought. She was used to friendly guests who wanted to chat, but Isabel Snyper seemed different, as though she wanted to pick Jane's brain.

"If you'll excuse me, I should clear the dining room table and start the dishwasher. I'm on a bit of a tight schedule today."

"Here I am, being a bother and taking up your valuable time. Let me help you."

"You're not a bother, not at all," Jane was quick to say. "One of the perks of running a bed-and-breakfast is getting to know interesting people. But you don't need to help. There's really not much left to do."

In spite of Jane's protest, Isabel followed her to the dining room and started gathering knives and forks.

"This is such a lovely room. It makes me feel transported back a hundred years. I've never seen Queen Anne–style dining room furniture used in such a charming setting. How many can you serve at the table?"

"When the leaves are in, it seats twelve comfortably." Jane turned off the coffee warmer on the buffet, but not before she offered Isabel another cup.

"No, thank you. I've already had three cups, far more than is usual for me. It was truly delicious. Do you add anything to it? I've heard of adding an egg white, but maybe that was only hearsay."

"No, it's pure coffee," Jane said. "I grind the beans myself. I've always thought the secret of good coffee is freshness, that and buying a good brand."

"You certainly don't skimp on what you serve your guests," Isabel said with admiration. "Where did you learn so much about cooking?"

"I trained as a professional chef."

"How interesting! I imagine any number of restaurants would be delighted to have you working for them."

"That's a phase of my career that I've left behind."

Jane had no intention of explaining that she'd once been married to a fellow chef whose professional jealousy had doomed their relationship. As a hostess in the inn, she was always willing to answer questions about their bed-and-breakfast, but she wasn't comfortable talking about herself with Mrs. Snyper. She remembered Louise's description of her experience with Mr. Snyper in the attic. They were certainly the most inquisitive couple who had ever stayed at the inn.

"I never could figure out how the chefs in a restaurant kitchen can keep track of a whole roomful of diners. It must have been a hectic existence compared to the slower pace of this inn." She barely paused to take a breath before jumping to another subject. "How do you handle guests who have food allergies and such? Has that ever been a problem?"

"Not really," Jane said. "If someone mentions an allergy, naturally we make sure they're not served anything that will trigger it."

"That is good of you. Are you open to preparing special breakfasts?"

"Guests usually trust us to serve something nice. Children are our severest critics, but we keep a supply of peanut butter and cereal for those youngsters who don't care for our regular offerings."

"Do many children stay here?"

"A few."

"How do you entertain them?"

"It's really not our responsibility."

"No, I suppose not, although the young ones must have a tendency to get into things. Do you have a list of babysitters for parents who want to get away from them for a while?"

"My sister Alice sponsors a group of young girls at church, the ANGELs. She knows reliable sitters, but again, it doesn't come up very often. Most of our guests just stay one or two nights unless they have family in town or a special event to attend."

"You probably wonder why we're staying so long," Isabel said in a tone that suggested she was willing to trade confidences.

Jane headed toward the kitchen with the plates and coffee cups, not sure how to answer. As it happened, she didn't need to.

"My husband's job is so stressful. We're seriously thinking of early retirement, but we can't afford to do it unless we live in a less expensive community. You might say we're scouting locations."

"We have some very happy retirees in Acorn Hill."

Jane was wondering how much longer Isabel would linger in the kitchen, when a man's voice arrested her attention.

Vern Snyper was standing in the kitchen doorway, a dapper straw hat perched on his head.

"Are you ready to go?" he asked his wife. "I've been waiting for you."

"Sorry, we've been having such a nice chat." She smiled broadly at Jane. "Thank you for putting up with all my questions."

"It's been a pleasure visiting with you."

Jane watched them go, a bit baffled by Isabel's abundant curiosity. Most guests appreciated the seamless hospitality of the inn, but she couldn't remember anyone who was so interested in the everyday workings of a bed-and-breakfast. Still, she'd been dealing with the public long enough to know that people came in infinite varieties. The Lord had made everyone unique, and that was part of what made her own life with others so richly satisfying.

Alice was delighted with the response she'd gotten so far to the wellness newsletter. Having Jody write up interviews would be wonderful, and there was no shortage of people willing to contribute their expertise. Still, Alice felt a vague apprehension about the interviews. It was one thing to enjoy talking to people and quite another to elicit enough information for a worthwhile article.

She did know one person who could help: Carlene Moss, the editor, photographer and business manager of Acorn Hill's weekly newspaper, the *Acorn Nutshell*. Alice phoned her during morning break, and Carlene agreed to give her some pointers on interviewing.

"Come to my house when you're through work today," Carlene said. "After I get the paper out on Wednesdays, I like to leave work early, kick off my shoes and relax."

Alice headed there directly after her shift, hoping to learn enough from Carlene to do a satisfactory job of interviewing.

Like the Howard sisters, Carlene lived in her childhood home, a pleasant bungalow on a tree-shaded street a block away from the sisters' friends Vera and Fred Humbert. She was virtually a one-woman staff at the paper where her father had once been the typesetter. She employed part-time help in selling advertising, printing and distributing the weekly, but she took responsibility for most of the content.

Alice found Carlene relaxing on the patio behind the house, shaded from the sun by a big green and yellow striped umbrella. She was barefoot and was sipping a glass of lemonade, looking totally at ease with the world. When she saw Alice, she smiled broadly, a dimple appearing in each cheek of her heart-shaped face. Her brown hair, somewhat coarse and unruly on the best of days, was swept up in a ponytail, and she wore a sleeveless yellow sundress.

"Alice, good to see you," she said, standing and walking toward her. "Come have some lemonade before the ice in the pitcher melts. It's unbelievable. This August has been a scorcher, and it's still only the first week."

"I'd love some. How have you been, Carlene?"

"Great. Amazingly, our little paper keeps increasing its circulation. The people in town want the local news that never shows up in bigger papers."

"That is good to hear." Alice sat down across from her at a round metal table that had been repainted lime green. The matching chairs were metal too, but thick seat pads with flowered canvas covers insulated them from the late afternoon heat.

"So you're going to be a reporter," Carlene teased.

"Hardly. The hospital wants to issue periodic wellness newsletters to encourage employees to stay healthy. I'm just one member of the committee—"

"And the one who's taking on the job of editor."

"Well, yes, I guess so, but what I don't know about putting a newsletter together is substantial. Fortunately it will be laid out and printed by the administration. My job is to find interesting topics."

"And write about them?"

"No, one of our younger nurses has volunteered for that, but she doesn't like to interview people. That's my job. I'm desperate for some pointers from a professional."

"You shouldn't have any trouble. You're naturally friendly and outgoing, but there are a few tips I can give you."

"I have a notebook in my purse," Alice said, searching in the big woven cotton bag she often carried in the summer. "One thing I already know is not to rely solely on memory."

"That would have been the first thing I'd tell you," Carlene said with a broad smile. "You might consider using a small tape recorder, but you have to tell the person about it. I always tape their permission to record."

"Then I won't need a notebook."

"Maybe. Maybe not. I make notes to myself during an interview, points to bring up, things to emphasize. It's a big help when it comes time to write the article."

"My helper, Jody Monroe, will be with me during interviews. Maybe one of us can have the recorder and the other the notebook."

"Sounds like a plan."

"I still need to know some basics."

"An interview is much like an ordinary conversation, but with more structure. I always prepare a list of questions ahead of time, although sometimes I junk them if my source says something more interesting than what I intended to ask. I don't know how many times I've gone after one story and discovered a better one by talking to the person."

"The source, that's the person you're interviewing?"

"Yes, and one thing that's really important is to make your source comfortable. Start with a little small talk. Show that you're truly interested in what they have to say. I suspect you'll do that naturally. I only mention it because it's important. You can't get a good story by putting the source on the defensive."

"So far it sounds like something I can do," Alice said thoughtfully.

"No question you can." Carlene pushed a bowl of peanuts toward her, but Alice shook her head. "Fortunately, people love to tell stories. Listening to them creates trust and helps break down reservations they might have about being interviewed."

Alice was taking notes to be sure she would remember everything Carlene was telling her.

"I like to interview people where the stories happen, their workplaces or the scenes of the action. It adds a little drama, even to routine articles. If I write that Grace Chapel will host an organ concert, I want to be in the church, hearing the organ and sensing how good the acoustics are. It gives me a feeling for its importance that I can't get over tea and cookies in a chairperson's home."

"In my case, that will mostly mean interviewing people in the hospital."

"That will work well. Finding some success stories, some testimonials, would be good too." Carlene poured more lemonade for herself, but Alice smiled and resisted a refill.

"Oh my, there's more of a technique to this than I suspected."

"I'll tell you what was hardest for me—learning when to be quiet. Sometimes a source needs a moment of quiet time to collect his or her thoughts. When I first started as a reporter, I thought that I needed to fill every second with conversation."

"That sounds exactly like what I would do," Alice said with a chuckle. "I think what you're telling me is to be a good listener, not just a questioner. Oh dear, I wonder whether I can do all this."

"You'll get the hang of it after a few interviews. One thing that I don't need to tell you is to be friendly. Some reporters I've met in my career are pretty abrasive. They think they can badger a source into giving something away. More likely the source will hunker down and refuse to respond.

People will want to talk to you, Alice, because you're always so pleasant."

"Thank you, but I still don't feel like a reporter."

"Well, you have to be something of an actor, I guess." Carlene laughed. "It's impossible to be bowled over by every little thing people say, but if you're polite and professional, they'll respond well to your questions most of the time. And fortunately for you, you're not trying to debunk anything."

"Maybe my biggest problem will be not understanding what some professionals say. I know quite a bit about health care in general, but little about some of the specialties related to wellness."

"Never be afraid to admit it. Some of my best stories came after I asked for explanations of things I didn't understand. People love to expound on what they know. I think there's something of a teacher in practically everyone. Be willing to be surprised. Sometimes the story comes from things you never suspected."

"Maybe I should have tape-recorded everything you've told me," Alice said, looking up from the pad of paper where she'd scribbled notes.

"Most of this will come naturally because you genuinely care about people. I know you would never let your personal feelings or biases shape a story. When you respect people, they want to help. Interviews usually go just fine when the reporter remembers to treat people the way he or she would like to be treated. But I'm preaching to the choir," Carlene said with a broad smile. "I can't imagine you acting any other way."

"You're sweet to say so," Alice said with a serene smile. "So many things come down to the Golden Rule, don't they?"

"That they do," Carlene agreed. "I'd love to see a copy of your newsletter when it comes out, if that would be okay with the hospital. Wellness is an important issue nationwide. I sometimes think I haven't given it enough attention in the *Nutshell.*"

"I'll be sure that you get one. Thank you so much for your help," Alice said, standing to leave. "I really appreciate it."

"Any time," Carlene said, getting up to walk Alice to her car. "I'd like to meet the nurse who's helping you. Maybe she would be willing to do a little freelance work for me if she has time. I always need writers to cover things that happen at the hospital."

"She's very hesitant about interviewing, but I'll certainly mention it to her."

"Anyone can learn to do an interview, but it is a handicap to be shy," Carlene said with understanding.

Alice drove home with ideas bouncing around in her head. The first thing she had to do to prepare for an interview was to find and learn to use a small handheld recorder. Then she had to make a list of questions, but Carlene had stressed that the person—the source—might say things that went well beyond any preplanned format.

The more Alice thought about it, the more it seemed like an adventure. She was bubbling over with enthusiasm and eager to share what she'd learned with her sisters.

Louise straightened the parlor after the last of her pupils had left. She felt pleased about the progress they'd made today. It had been a good sign that most had opted to continue their lessons during the summer break from school, so she wasn't surprised by the positive results. The only exception was Charley LaCroix. He seemed to resent the time he spent with her, and she was at a loss about how to encourage him. Maybe his mother would have some suggestions when she arrived for a conference. Unfortunately, Louise wasn't optimistic.

As she pushed the bench closer to the piano, she noticed a small hair pick on the floor. It must have fallen from one of the girls' purses or pockets. She picked it up, intending to put it in the box she kept on a closet shelf. Now that she thought of it, her lost and found collection had grown quite a bit over the summer. She really should set it out so her pupils could claim some of their missing items.

She busied herself for a few more minutes, waiting for the parent to arrive. Mrs. LaCroix had called early in the day asking to see her. She didn't give a reason, but Louise could guess. No doubt she was unhappy with her son's progress, but there was little Louise could do without some cooperation from him. She'd been debating with herself all day over whether or not to drop him as a pupil. She still hadn't decided.

"Hello, you said to walk right in," Mrs. LaCroix said from the doorway.

"Yes, please do come in."

Louise had arranged two of the Eastlake chairs to face each other over a small occasional table. It was a formal but still comfortable setting for a meeting.

"If you'd like to sit," she said gesturing.

"This is such a pretty room," Mrs. LaCroix said. "You and your sisters must be into collecting. The curio cabinets, the antique dolls, the brass mantel clock. So many lovely things."

"We're more curators of family keepsakes than collectors," Louise said, sensing that Mrs. LaCroix wasn't sure how to begin the conversation about her son.

"I don't want to take a lot of your time."

She sat squeezing her hands together on her lap, and Louise couldn't help noticing that she had exceptionally long, slender fingers. Her jet black hair was swept back into a tight bun, and her pale blue slacks had a sharp crease. Her blouse, which appeared to be silk, was high necked with long sleeves and a touch of lace at the wrists. Like Charley, she was tall and quite thin, and it seemed to be difficult for her to sit still.

"What can I tell you about Charley's lessons? I'm afraid he isn't making as much progress as he might."

"Yes, that's my concern. The blunt truth is, Mrs. Smith, that he doesn't seem to be making any progress at all. Our whole family is musical. I was a concert pianist in my younger days, and my husband plays his violin in a chamber music group. Charley's sister is studying music education at the university. I know my son has the ability. He's shown great promise since he was a toddler."

"I'm sure he doesn't lack ability," Louise said.

"We tried him on the violin, then the cello when he was big enough. It's probably my fault for not starting his piano lessons sooner, but my husband felt sure Charley would follow in his footsteps on a string instrument."

"Does he still play the cello?" This was news to Louise.

"No, at least not this summer. We decided he needed a rest from it."

Judging from the grass-stained baseball that Charley usually brought to his lessons, Louise guessed that his mind was on activities that had nothing to do with music. She had considered dropping him, since he was, at best, indifferent to his lessons. She wouldn't at all mind if his mother stopped them, but she wondered whether Charley had had a say.

"Have you asked your son if there's any musical instrument he would like to play?"

Mrs. LaCroix looked startled but quickly recovered her composure.

"Oh, I suspect he'd like to play a guitar or some rock-band instrument, but that would be such a waste of his talent. His father doesn't want him spending time on that sort of thing."

Louise breathed deeply, her sympathy wholly with young Charley now.

"The crux of the matter is that Charley won't be coming to you for more piano lessons. We're looking for a teacher in Potterston."

Louise should have been relieved to be done with a problem student, but she felt sure that the boy would be equally unresponsive and miserable with another teacher.

"May I speak frankly, Mrs. LaCroix?" Louise asked gently.

She visibly stiffened but nodded assent.

"I don't think Charley will be successful on any instrument unless he chooses one that interests him. It seems that he has the ability, but he's at an age where he's trying to discover who he is and what he wants to do with his life. It's your decision, of course, but I urge you to talk to him before you sign him up for more lessons. He might surprise you."

"We've always communicated with our son," she said defensively.

"But have you considered what he wants to do?"

Louise suspected that she'd gone too far, but she'd never known a reluctant student to become an accomplished one.

"Charley won't be coming to you for lessons anymore," Mrs. LaCroix said, standing to leave. "I'm sure you did the best you could, but obviously you weren't able to stimulate his interest."

When Charley's mother was gone, Louise sat at the piano for some time, idly picking out notes without actually playing anything. She couldn't regret losing the boy as a pupil, but the idea of forcing any child to play an instrument made her sad. She thanked the Lord that her daughter Cynthia loved music. It had forged a bond between them that went beyond their blood ties, but if it had been other-wise, would she have insisted that she play an instrument?

It was unlikely she would see Charley again except as a boy riding his bike through town, but she felt a curious sense of loss. Somewhere under his rebellious exterior, there might be a musician trying to break loose. She could only pray for him as she did for all the children who came to her for lessons. And she prayed for herself as well, hoping that she hadn't done more harm than good by speaking her mind to his mother.

Chapter Four

"Can you imagine walking from Nebraska to New York?" Jane said as she pored over their reservations on Thursday morning. "No wonder that guest is running a day late. He canceled his reservation for last night, but said he hoped to get here tonight. He didn't want to tie up a room in case he couldn't make it, but I assured him that we would have an opening. In fact, as it stands now, we have two."

Louise had just gathered some supplies and was on her way to clean the parlor, a room that she felt was her responsibility just as Jane was responsible for all that needed to be done in the kitchen.

"Goodness, I can't even imagine going that far on foot. Why is he doing it?"

"When he phoned for the original reservation, he mentioned his enthusiasm for hiking and biking trails. He's encouraging towns on his route to provide safe, convenient walkways so everyone can enjoy all that nature has to offer.

I'm eager to meet him, so I hope he makes it tonight. I guess he got delayed somewhere along the way. He wasn't absolutely sure of his time, but I have my fingers crossed that he'll get here. I don't think we've ever had a rash of cancellations like this. Another party backed out—again for a good reason. Their daughter went into premature labor, so they decided to fly to be with her instead of stopping here and having a leisurely drive to Baltimore."

"I'm sure it's coincidence that so many have canceled in a few short weeks, but if it keeps up, perhaps we'll have to rethink our advertising."

"We've done so well with our online listing, not to mention word of mouth," Jane said wistfully. "I'm not sure what's going on."

"It's a problem," Louise said frowning. "We want to keep our rooms full, but we only have four to offer. Advertising in a national publication might swamp us with requests that we can't honor."

"We don't need to decide now," Jane said. "As you pointed out, it's probably only coincidence that we've had several people back out."

Louise went toward the parlor, but she didn't get far. Mr. and Mrs. Snyper came down the stairs and started talking to her.

"My, but you ladies look ambitious this morning," Isabel said, dressed today in a short-sleeved peach silk shirt and beige linen slacks. "I do admire how clean you keep your place. We've stayed in some lovely hotels, but I don't think any of them were as spick-and-span as Grace Chapel Inn."

"That's nice to hear," Louise said, since the remark was addressed to her. "Fortunately, we adore the house, and it's a labor of love to keep it sparkling clean."

"I can imagine how you must feel. I take a great deal of pride in our little house, although I have to confess that I have a housekeeper who comes two days a week. Not that I think cleaning is beneath me, but my decorating business keeps me running. Tell me, do you do all the yard work yourself, or do you have a service for that?"

"We do most of it," Louise said. "Jane is a wonder at gardening."

"Yes, we had a look at your garden yesterday. Is there a nursery nearby where you buy your annuals?"

"We have several," Jane said.

"Say, I have a question," Vern said. "If guests arrive without their own transportation, do you provide shuttle service back and forth to the airport or train station?"

"No, we're just a small operation," Jane explained. "I don't think there's ever been a situation where we were asked to give taxi service."

"I was just curious," he said with a faint smile. "We usually drive, of course, so it wouldn't influence our decision to stay here."

"Well, we're off," Isabel said, taking her husband's arm, then thinking of something else she wanted to say. "By the way, I love the little shell-shaped soaps in our bathroom, so much nicer than the miniature bars in motels, but I couldn't tell what brand they are."

"They're homemade," Jane said. "I bought a supply at a craft show in the spring. I was attracted by the lovely pastel colors. I'm glad to hear you enjoy using them."

"I imagine there's a lot of waste in your business. What can you do with the used soaps?"

"Well, regulations say they can't be reused by other guests. That's why we use the little shells instead of big bars, but I do put the remnants in a big jar with a small amount of water." Jane said. "When they dissolve, it becomes a cleaning solution and can also be used in the laundry. I especially like to use it for throw rugs."

"How clever," Isabel said. "I imagine little economies like that make a difference in your profit margin."

"I doubt that it's substantial," Jane said, "but we like to recycle wherever possible."

"Very admirable," Vern said. "What if a guest forgets something essential like toothpaste or shaving cream?"

"Or maybe a shower cap or moisturizer," his wife chimed in.

"I guess we've been lucky with our guests. It rarely comes up, but we do have sample sizes of various products, as well as disposable showercaps, and there is a pharmacy within easy walking distance."

"It's so nice to be able to walk to stores," Isabel said. "Exercise and convenience all in one. I can't tell you how much I'm enjoying your town. I could spend hours in that wonderful little bookstore. What was the name?" she asked her husband.

"I forget. Something offbeat," he said. "It's a lot more convenient at a place like that to ask for what you want instead of wandering around in one of the big chain stores. Of course, a small store can stock only so much."

"It's Nine Lives Bookstore," Louise said, answering Isabel's question. "The owner, Viola Reed, is extremely fond of cats. That's where the name comes from."

"I assume you don't allow animals in the inn," Isabel said. "So many people are allergic to cats and such."

"Are you?" Jane asked.

"Oh no, I tolerate them, but I don't like it when they climb all over everything."

"Actually, we do have a cat, Wendell, but he usually keeps out of the way of guests," Jane admitted.

"I hope you don't allow him on your kitchen counter. My cousin is cat-crazy. She thinks nothing of letting hers on the kitchen table and work spaces while she's cooking. I find it very unsanitary."

"Wendell knows his place," Louise said firmly, "and it certainly isn't on counters."

"I didn't mean to imply—"

"We'd better get going," her husband said, cutting her off and taking her arm.

"Yes, of course. Well, have a nice day. I really do admire how clean you keep the inn."

Jane and Louise watched them go and then looked at each other. Louise stood with a hand on her hip, raising one eyebrow in an expression of puzzlement.

"They certainly ask a lot of questions," she said. "You were right about that."

"We've never had guests that curious," Jane said. "Do you suppose they probe into everything wherever they go?"

"Maybe it's their way of being friendly." Louise didn't sound as though she believed it.

"It's not as if they complain. On the contrary, they're usually very complimentary. They seem to appreciate the inn quite a bit. Sometimes I feel as though they're prospective buyers, not just ordinary guests. But I guess that's silly."

"It is a little odd, though," Louise said. "Usually when people are interested in striking up a friendship, they ask more personal questions."

"Like where I trained to be a chef or what your musical background is. All their questions have to do with how we run the inn."

"Curious," Louise said shaking her head as she moved toward the parlor to do her cleaning.

Jane agreed, but maybe the Snypers took a special interest in how things worked. It was rather unusual for three sisters to be in business together, especially since they did it in such obvious harmony.

Mr. Harris was busted. Alice was hard put to suppress a smile, but she was relieved that the elderly gentleman's heart pains had such a simple explanation. He'd passed all his tests, and now, this afternoon, he was ready to go home after his trip to the emergency room.

"I can't believe you went to a fast-food place," his wife scolded. "I left a perfectly nice breakfast warming in the oven for you." She turned to Alice for support. "I can't even go to a Garden Club breakfast meeting without him getting into trouble."

"You can't expect a man to live on mush," he grumbled. "And it wasn't fast food. The Knife and Fork serves good, wholesome meals."

"You'll give me a heart attack, gobbling down greasy fried potatoes with onions."

"And bacon bits," he said with a mischievous smile. "I'd almost forgotten how bacon tastes."

"That would be bad enough," his wife went on, venting anger because she'd had a major scare when her husband doubled over with what appeared to be heart pains. "Whatever possessed you to order an omelet with green and red peppers? You know they give you heartburn."

"Hadn't had any problems in a long time. Anyway, it was a vegetarian omelet. I thought you'd approve."

"What can I do with this man?" she asked Alice in a tone of exasperated affection. "I try hard to serve only healthy food, but I don't get much cooperation."

"Maybe the two of you would like to see the hospital nutritionist together," Alice suggested. "She's a wonder when it comes to adding taste and appeal to healthy meals based on things a patient likes."

"No, thank you," Mrs. Harris said, sounding a trifle miffed. "I've been cooking for this man for over fifty years, and I have enough recipes to last a lifetime. It wasn't anything I made that brought him here."

"That's true," Alice agreed. "It was only a suggestion."

Her sympathy was with Mr. Harris. Listening to his complaints, she'd gathered that his diet was monotonous and bland: cooked cereal with skim milk and artificial sweetener for breakfast every morning, lots of steamed vegetables, brown rice, chicken and fish with servings of canned fruit or sugar-free pudding. His wife was extremely health-conscious, but she hadn't mastered the art of making nutritious food tasty and interesting.

The couple left the emergency area, and Alice turned her attention to the next patient. He hadn't been in Potterston Hospital before, so there wasn't a chart, only the information gathered at the reception desk. She went out to collect him in the waiting room.

"Perry Clay Garfield," she said reading his name out loud.

"Here, ma'am."

A tall, lanky young man with a mop of bright yellow-blond hair prepared to rise from the wheelchair that had been provided for him. He had startlingly bright blue eyes and a ruddy complexion sprinkled with freckles. He was dressed in a long-sleeved white T-shirt with a bright red cotton bandanna around his neck, threadbare jeans faded to pale blue and athletic shoes scuffed to a nondescript color. He picked up the wide-brimmed straw cowboy hat that sat on a soiled and battered yellow backpack, then stood and hoisted the pack on his shoulders.

"You didn't need to get up. I can push you in to see the doctor," Alice said, knowing that the receptionist wouldn't have seated him in a wheelchair without a good reason.

"Thank you, ma'am, but I can handle a few more steps."

Alice believed in picking her battles, and wrestling a strapping young patient into a chair wasn't going to be one of them.

She led him to one of the yellow-curtained examining cubicles, seated him on the table and read over the notes on his information sheet.

"Blisters," she said. "Take off your shoes and socks, and I'll have a look."

"They're not a pretty sight," he said with a sheepish grin. "My brother says I have the ugliest feet on a humanoid, and that's without a new crop of blisters."

"We don't give prizes for pretty toes," she said with a smile.

He dropped first one shoe, then the other beside the table, followed by moist, soiled tube socks. He winced a bit as he bared his feet.

Alice took one look and let out an unprofessional "Wow!" He had one of the worst case of blisters she'd ever seen, most of them on the soles of his feet. Worse, there were angry red streaks leading away from the severest of them, a sure sign that they were infected.

She was authorized to treat blisters when all they needed was some moleskin protection, but this was definitely a case for the doctor.

"Just relax," she said. "The doctor will be in as soon as he's free."

Dr. Garcia, an especially pleasant young resident, was on duty in the emergency room today. He was busy with a construction worker who'd come in with his eye bandaged from a work-related accident. Apparently it was a case for a specialist, and an ophthalmologist was on the way.

As soon as he was free, Alice directed him to the next patient, Perry Clay Garfield.

"Looks like you've put a lot of miles on those feet," Dr. Garcia said when he'd examined them.

"All the way from Omaha, Nebraska."

That caught both Alice's and the busy doctor's attention.

"You walked from Nebraska to Pennsylvania?" she asked in surprise.

"Yes, ma'am. I'm on my way to New York."

"Well, I'm afraid you've just hit a roadblock," Dr. Garcia said, studying with dark brown eyes and furrowed brows the patient's feet.

"Yeah, I was expecting that."

"I can drain the worst ones and bandage them with antibiotic ointment, but you'll have to do some healing before you get on your way."

Alice helped the doctor by washing the feet thoroughly with antibiotic soap and water while he prepared to puncture the worst blisters with a sterile needle.

"Most of them are large enough that they need to be drained," Dr. Garcia said. Inserting a needle into a huge blister on the ball of one foot, he frowned at the putrid yellow fluid draining out, another sign of infection.

"You've got yourself some infected blisters," he said shaking his head and continuing to drain them, sometimes applying gentle pressure with his gloved finger to force out the fluid. "Your foot is hot to the touch, and those red streaks are a negative sign."

"Did you walk here to the hospital?" Alice asked, wondering how anyone could take a step on such painful-looking feet.

"Yes, ma'am." The young man winced at the doctor's probing but didn't protest.

Dr. Garcia took his time, making light conversation to distract the patient as he worked. It was one of the reasons Alice liked working with him. He always considered the patient's feelings as well as the physical symptoms.

"Tell me more about this long walk of yours," he said.

"I'm sponsored by an environmental group in Nebraska, although I'm mostly using money my grandmother left me. She taught high school biology, and now my parents are with the University of Nebraska at Lincoln. Dad's a zoologist and Mom's a botanist. I don't have much of a head for their sciences, but I love the outdoors. I'm walking to promote hiking and biking trails. If people would get outside and enjoy nature, they'd have a better idea of what we're losing by poor stewardship of the earth."

Although he'd probably recited this hundreds of times on his hike, he spoke with passionate enthusiasm. Alice found herself wanting to know more about this mission of his, but for the moment, she was much too busy with the treatment and bandaging.

"Let's take a look at your shoes," the doctor said, bending over to scoop one up after he finished his part of the treatment. "I do some running, so I know how important the right shoes are."

In fact, Alice knew, Dr. Garcia was a marathon runner who kept trim and healthy with regular morning runs. The whole staff had been excited for him when he did well in the last Boston Marathon.

"I've been meaning to stop and buy a new pair, but I thought there were a few more miles in these."

"Well, Perry—"

"I generally go by Clay."

"Clay, I think it should be your number-one priority to get some better footwear. You might consider hiking boots. They give your feet more protection on a long walk."

Alice could see that the lining of the shoe was gray and tattered, worn away in patches and generally unsavory.

"And your socks," the doctor said.

He picked up one of them, for which Alice gave him great credit. It was pretty much a soggy mess.

"I always get nice heavy cotton ones," Clay said.

"The trouble with cotton is that it retains moisture, one of the big causes of blisters. Your feet get hot and perspire. That causes a lot of friction. When the surface layer of skin separates from the second layer, fluid fills the space between them and creates blisters."

"So my socks are actually causing blisters, not just my shoes. I've always believed cotton was the perfect material. What kind should I wear?"

"Choose a synthetic fabric. It won't retain moisture as easily. Stop often to change. When you wash your feet to cool off, be sure they're completely dry before you put your socks back on. The good news is that blisters are mostly preventable."

"What's the bad news?" Clay asked with a little half-grin.

"I want you to take a break from walking until the infection clears up. I'll give you a prescription, and you'll need to keep all the blistered areas covered. Apply a little antibiotic ointment whenever you change bandages. If the infection gets worse, call me." He took a small white business card out of a supply drawer and handed it to his patient. "I think your feet will heal in good order if you take proper care of them for a few days."

"I'm already a day behind schedule," the walker said unhappily. "A big thunderstorm in Iowa slowed me down."

"Trust me, you'll lose a lot more time if you don't get your feet in shape," Dr. Garcia said sympathetically. "I've had enough blisters myself to know that they don't get better overnight. When you do start walking again, put some moleskin on the most sensitive spots to cut down on friction."

"You've convinced me," he said. "I won't walk anywhere until they're better—except to Acorn Hill."

"I don't think you want to do that," the doctor said grimly, perhaps a little put out that his message hadn't sunk in.

"Why are you going to Acorn Hill?" Alice asked, wondering if he was one of the wayward guests Jane had been talking about.

"A nice lady at the bed-and-breakfast there promised me a room tonight. I had to cancel last night, and I don't want to let her down again."

"You came to the right place," Alice said. "There's only one bed-and-breakfast in Acorn Hill. My two sisters and I run it. I'm nearly through with my shift. You can ride there with me."

"That's awfully nice of you to offer, ma'am, but I'm committed to walking all the way. I wouldn't want to let down my sponsors by accepting a ride, even if I did already pass Acorn Hill to get here."

"There's no way you can make it back to Acorn Hill on those feet," Dr. Garcia said as he started to leave the cubicle. "Tell your sponsors that it was doctor's orders."

Clay thanked him profusely but still looked unhappy.

"Tell you what," Alice said. "Go down to the cafeteria and have a cold drink. I'll meet you there in about ten minutes. You can let me know then whether you want to ride with me."

"Fair enough. I do have a powerful thirst."

A few minutes later Alice checked out and collected her purse from her locker, half expecting the young walker to be gone when she went to meet him. Somewhat to her relief, he was seated at a table in the nearly empty room talking on his cell phone.

He broke off the call and grinned sheepishly as she walked over to him.

"I checked in with Omaha," he explained. "The managing director of our group gave me my marching orders—or rather my sitting orders. She doesn't think it will hurt our campaign for more and better hiking trails if I ride to Acorn Hill and stay put for a few days. In fact, she insisted. She doesn't want me thumping into the Big Apple on crutches."

"She sounds like a wise woman," Alice said. "We can leave now. It's a bit of a walk to my car."

She wanted to suggest getting a wheelchair for him but sensed that he might take offense. Even elderly patients sometimes resented not being allowed to leave under their own power.

"I'm obliged for the ride, ma'am."

"Please call me Alice. I'm eager to hear about some of your experiences. You must have seen some beautiful country."

"Crossing the Mississippi was my favorite," he said limping beside her as they left. "There's an overlook on the Illinois side. I must've spent an hour there watching the river traffic. Couldn't help wondering where the barges had been and where they were going. Reminded me of how much I like reading Mark Twain. I've got *Life on the Mississippi* in my backpack, not that I've had much time for it. Generally I'm asleep as soon as I stop for the night. One of my goals is to walk along the river from its source in Minnesota to New Orleans. I feel like the river is an old friend because I've read Mark Twain's accounts of it so many times."

"I haven't thought about him in a long time," Alice said. "I remember reading *Tom Sawyer*. Who could ever forget how he convinced other boys to whitewash the fence for him?"

"That was cool. I guess I've read about everything he wrote, but I think his earlier stuff is better. I read *The Celebrated Jumping Frog of Calaveras County* when I was in middle school. I've been hooked on his stories ever since. He didn't just make them up. He lived them. His father died when he was only twelve, and he went to work for a printer. Guess that's how he got interested in writing. He was younger than I was when he started working on the river and got his pilot's license. That's how he picked his pseudonym, you know."

"I remember something about it. His real name was Samuel Clemens, wasn't it?"

Alice couldn't help noticing that Clay was walking gingerly, obviously in some pain. She moved slowly so that he could keep up.

"Yeah, he picked Mark Twain because it was a river term for two fathoms or twelve feet. The water had to be at least that deep for safe navigation. It's still a tricky waterway."

"You're not tempted to go by river instead of on foot?"

"No, I like the freedom of the road. If I want to spend a week in Hannibal, Missouri, I can. His house there has been turned into a museum, you know."

"Yes, I think I've heard that. Here's my car," she said, opening the door for her passenger.

"It's funny, you know," he said, somehow folding his length into her small compact. "His frog story was published nearly a hundred and forty years ago, and it's still a hoot. People don't change all that much, only not many kids have the kind of freedom Huck Finn had."

"No, they do sensible things like go to school," Alice teased, surprised at how much at ease she felt with this young stranger.

"I have done that," he said with a chuckle. "I didn't want to disappoint my parents, so I got a degree in environmental science. Turns out I loved it, but I got a second major in English lit. I have it in the back of my mind that someday I'll be a writer. For now, I only keep a journal of my travels. I'm afraid I'll have to work a couple of years before my next long trip, though. My grandmother's legacy won't last forever, and I had to use a lot of it to pay off my college loans."

"What kind of job are you looking at?" she asked, pulling out of the hospital parking lot.

"Well, my parents are pushing graduate school, but I want to have some experience before I figure out what I want to do. For now I'm really into hiking. Whenever I can, I stop and talk up how great it is to be able to walk or bike on nature trails. If even one town lays out a trail because of my trek, I'll feel that it's a big success. I don't have the credentials for city planning or teaching, but I love outdoor work. Maybe I could do landscaping or agricultural projects, although I've done more than my share of detasseling."

"Detasseling?"

"Ever since I was old enough, I've spent my summers detasseling corn. That's how they get seeds for hybrid corn. Machines can only get about seventy percent of the tassels, so there's a lot of handwork involved."

"What exactly does that involve?"

"You just pull off the top of the cornstalks, the tassels, and drop them on the ground. Every other row is a different kind of corn. When the tassels are pulled from one row, the pollen from the rows next to it pollinates those stalks. That makes the seed corn more productive. Some kids think it's boring or too hard, just going up and down the rows all day pulling off tassels, but I could make more in the six-week season than I could working all summer at a fast-food place. It gave me spending money and time to do other things."

"It does sound like hard work," Alice said. "Is this your first long walk?

"Pretty much so, but I've biked across Iowa. Every summer they have an event called RAGBRAI—The Des Moines Register's Annual Great Bicycle Ride Across Iowa. Thousands of people ride across the state. My parents let me go alone when I was only fourteen, and I've gone quite a few times since. All the little towns along the way offer hospitality. It's great, really. One big party, and you really get to see the state."

"I don't know that I've ever met an adventurer like you."

Alice was thinking of her dear friend Mark Graves, a big-animal vet who now worked at the Philadelphia Zoo. In college they'd had a close relationship, but their differing goals had pulled them apart. Since renewing their friendship, she'd been impressed at all the worldwide experiences he'd had, but he'd always worked for an organization that sponsored his work abroad. This young man's travels were quite different. He went alone but seemed to have great zest for seeing new places.

"You'd be surprised how many people are on the move all over the country," he said. "Much as I enjoy the sights, it's the folks I meet along the way who make it worthwhile.

I treat myself to a nice place like your bed-and-breakfast from time to time, but I don't know how many times I've enjoyed the hospitality of strangers. In fact, I've never had a farmer refuse to let me sleep in his barn."

"Don't you ever get lonely?"

"Oh no, ma'am. I'm never alone."

"You've been traveling with someone?"

"The Lord Jesus is with me every step. I like to think He enjoys seeing some of God's creation as we go along. He was quite a walker Himself, you know."

Alice didn't answer. Her eyes misted over with wonder at the faith of the young man beside her.

Chapter Five

*J*ane was pleased when Alice brought their new guest to the inn, but she was sorry to see him limping badly when he came in.

"Jane, this is Perry Clay Garfield. I gave him a ride from the hospital since the doctor vetoed the idea of walking here on blistered feet."

"Welcome to Grace Chapel Inn, Mr. Garfield."

"Just call me Clay, ma'am," he said offering his hand. "I'm much obliged to Miss Alice for bringing me here. This is such a pretty town, all the big trees and gardens. People here must care a lot about it to keep it so beautiful."

"Thank you, Clay. People here do take pride in their town," Jane responded.

After checking in, their latest guest asked, "Do you have a hiking trail in Acorn Hill?"

"Not a formal hiking trail. There are some nice side roads, a lovely trail not far from here at a place called Fairy Pond, and, of course, a lot of people take daily walks around the town."

"I imagine it's a nice place to walk."

"We think so." Jane smiled. "If you like, I'll show you up to your room, Clay."

"No need to trouble yourself, ma'am. Just point me in the right direction."

"It's no trouble." She fetched the key and started up, hard-pressed not to wince when she looked behind her and saw him limping up the stairs.

"I've put you in the Sunrise Room, the back room on the right," Jane said. "As I told you on the phone, it does share a bath with one other room. Tonight that one will be occupied by a salesman who stays here quite often. He'll leave early in the morning, so he shouldn't be in your way."

"No problem. The Sunrise Room. That must mean it gets the morning sun," he said, limping his way to the door. "That will suit me perfectly. That's the way God wakes us up. I didn't even bother bringing an alarm clock with me."

She opened the door and handed him the key. He walked right past the furnishings and the big landscape painting on the wall and went to the window that looked down on the garden.

"Nice," he said, more to himself than to her. "I hope you don't mind if I have a shower before I go out for dinner. I expect you folks are having to conserve water, judging by how burnt some of the lawns are."

"So far the ban only applies to sprinklers, so by all means, use what you need," Jane said. "I have a better idea about dinner though. Why not eat with us tonight?"

"I don't want to intrude. I understand that breakfast is the only meal that comes with the room."

"It is, but my sister Alice won't hear of you walking around town on freshly treated blisters. You're our guest this evening, and I have to admit, I'd love to hear about your trip. Nebraska! That sounds like the end of the world when I think of walking all the way from there."

"Then it would be my pleasure to join you, ma'am."

He had a boyish grin that made his otherwise homely face light up.

"Dinner will be ready around six, and please do call me Jane."

"Just give a holler, if you would please, Jane."

She smiled all the way back to the kitchen. This guest hardly noticed whether there was a bed in his room, but he seemed to fit in like an old friend. Maybe the cancellation had had a purpose. If the other guests had showed up as planned, the sisters wouldn't have been able to accommodate Clay tonight.

Jane went back to the kitchen wondering how to stretch dinner enough to allow for a young man's appetite. She couldn't help but notice that he was thin, no doubt burning calories like mad as he walked all day. She wasn't a cook who delighted in "fattening up" anyone who came her way, but she didn't want him to leave her table still hungry.

Ethel had already been invited to join them for dinner, so Jane had planned a light meal to fit the dog days of summer. She'd already made a chicken salad with green grapes and walnuts, a family favorite, but divided five ways it would make a skimpy meal for the young man.

She stared hard at the interior of the freezer, but nothing in her ample supply of food inspired her. The fridge was equally uninspiring until she spotted the remnants of a large ham roll. She'd been gradually using it to add protein to her breakfasts, but there was more than enough left for ham croquettes. Her favorite recipe called for adding crushed graham crackers, which would extend the ham enough to serve all of them.

She chuckled to herself at what the chefs who'd taught her would say about serving ham croquettes with chicken salad, but she had enough fresh green beans to make a buffer between them. On short notice, it was the best she could do without eliminating the salad, one of Ethel's favorites.

Ethel arrived early, looking pert in a pretty pink sundress with a matching jacket. Jane was grateful for her help in setting the dining room table. She briefly mentioned the extra guest but didn't explain why he was having dinner with the family. Her aunt would have dozens of questions, and Jane was too hard-pressed finishing her dinner preparations to answer them now. Anyway, little that she could say about Perry Clay Garfield would prepare Ethel for their unusual guest.

Louise had a surprise visitor. Charley appeared at the front door, knocking timidly. When she invited him to come inside, he declined, standing first on one foot, then the other and fiddling with the string of a yo-yo he held in his hand.

"May I help you with something, Charley?" she asked after an awkward moment of silence.

"You already have," he mumbled without looking directly at her. "I just wanted you to know something."

He shoved the yo-yo into the pocket of his jeans but still didn't look at her.

"Yes," Louise said to encourage him.

"I didn't want to quit piano because of you. I mean, I like you fine. That wasn't why I didn't want more lessons."

"I understand. I was sorry to lose you as a pupil, Charley, but the piano isn't for everyone."

"Thanks to you, my mom is going to let me play the trumpet. I'm going to be in the band when school starts." He smiled so happily that Louise was delighted for him.

"That's wonderful! I'll look forward to hearing you play."

"We'll play for football games and parades and I don't know what all. I'll get my uniform the first week of school, and the band director is really cool. He said if I take some private lessons and practice at home, I'll be able to catch up with the rest of the trumpet players in a hurry. I want to be first chair when I get to high school."

"I'd be very surprised if you weren't," she said smiling back at him.

"Well, that's all I wanted to tell you. I have to get home for supper," he said, turning to bound down the porch steps. When he got to the bottom, he turned and gave her a wave. "Bye, Mrs. Smith."

Louise beamed as he jumped on his bike and rode away. Losing a student had never felt so good.

By the time she freshened up for dinner, everyone had gathered in the dining room, although no one was seated yet. They had a guest she didn't know, but Ethel was quick to make the introductions.

"This is Perry Clay Garfield," she said, her cheeks pink with excitement. "Can you believe it? He walked here all the way from Nebraska, and he's going to keep going until he gets to New York."

"That's quite an accomplishment, Mr. Garfield. I am pleased to meet you."

"My pleasure, ma'am, but my friends call me Clay."

"I'm Louise, and I see that you've already met my sisters."

"Ms. Jane was kind enough to ask me to supper. And Miss Alice gave me a ride from Potterston. The Lord was surely smiling on me when He brought me to your part of the country."

"Well, I hope you enjoy your stay with us," Louise said.

Her first impression was that she'd never met anyone quite like the walker. He talked and looked like a country boy, and he had a natural charm that drew people to him almost immediately. It was soon obvious that he was exceptionally bright, but he was humble and listened with great courtesy to everything that was said.

When Jane finished bringing in the food, he asked if he could say the blessing, and before anyone realized what was happening, he had them standing around the table with joined hands.

"Dear Lord, You've brought me to this table with these good people. I thank You from the bottom of my heart and ask Your blessing on all assembled here. Let there always be faith and love in their lives. Thank You for the bounty of this meal, and let us always remember those who are less fortunate. Amen."

Louise joined in saying "Amen," then took a place to the left of their young guest. Ethel sat on his right, giggling a bit when he held the chair for her. Alice and Jane sat across from them, beaming approval at his courtly treatment of their aunt. He had a gift for being congenial, and they were glad that he was giving Ethel special attention.

"Have you run into any dangers on your walk?" Ethel asked when they'd all helped themselves to the dishes that were passed around the table. "I can't imagine walking along one of those busy expressways."

"I try to avoid them," Clay said, eating hungrily but not paying much attention to the food. "I like walking through smaller towns, and, of course, talking to folks about laying out trails so everyone has a pleasant, safe way to enjoy nature."

"It must be quite expensive to acquire enough land and pave a trail," Louise said.

"There are ways it can be done. Deserted railway lines make great trails with the tracks removed. Some landowners will donate a right-of-way across their property. Sometimes volunteers will clear the land. There's always a way, but it takes a lot of determination and commitment."

"It sounds like something the government should be doing with our money," Ethel said.

"They get involved at all levels," Clay assured her. "And trails aren't limited to greenbelts circling cities. My cousin lives in Clive, Iowa, near Des Moines, and I've walked their trail several times with him. It winds its way along a creek through some beautiful wooded areas. There are markers to identify trees, wildflowers and such."

"I would love that," Jane said.

"Not only that, it links existing parks and recreation areas. A few sections even use streets and sidewalks along the way. In one place it enters a shopping district. But the best part is that the Clive greenbelt links to other trails. One extension links it to a fifty-seven-mile trail in the Raccoon River Valley. Even more extensions are planned. Imagine being able to hike or bike for hundreds of miles."

In his enthusiasm, he'd forgotten about eating.

"I love the idea of a whole community out walking and enjoying the natural beauty right near their homes," Jane said.

"Not only that," Alice said, "imagine how much it contributes to people's health and wellness if they spend leisure time hiking or biking."

"It's a win-win idea any way you look at it," Louise agreed.

"When the snow piles up, trails also make good places for cross-country skiing," he said.

"I like the idea that you can walk a long way or just stroll along and visit with friends," Ethel said.

"I imagine it's a good way to get children outdoors and let them see how interesting nature is," Louise said, thinking of the mad dashes the local boys made through town on their bikes. "Safer, too, than riding bicycles on the streets."

"Did you see any dangerous wildlife on your way here?" Ethel asked. "I was thinking of the kind that bite and sting."

"The grasshoppers were out in eastern Iowa. They can be sort of annoying, but it is fun to watch them jump. Reminded me of locust plagues in the Bible. One lady at a convenience store said they ruined a few screens at her home last year. Bit right through the wire mesh. Fortunately they aren't plentiful enough this year to hurt the crops."

"I was thinking more of snakes," Ethel admitted. "All those years on my farm, and I never did get over being afraid of them."

"I saw a few," Clay said, "but man is much more danger-ous to them than they are to us. Most that I saw had been run over on the road. They're pretty shy as a rule, although my cousin in Clive, Jimmy, did have a run-in with a rattler."

"In Iowa?" Jane asked. "I always thought of them living in the West."

"Well, this one was right in the middle of a hiking trail when my cousin was out running. It was shaking rattles like crazy and poised to strike. Happens he was in a park, and there was a bench along the side of the trail. He picked up the bench—I guess his adrenaline was really high because it had cast-iron legs and hardwood slats—and threw it at the snake. Then he jumped over it and ran like crazy. Never did look back to see what happened to the snake."

"My, I've never heard of dealing with a snake that way," Ethel said with a gasp. "Do you suppose he crushed it?"

"I hope he just confused it," Clay said. "After all, a snake is one of God's creatures too. I think I would've just stood there waiting for it to go away."

"Do you think it's wrong to kill any animal?" Ethel asked, squinting to look at his plate, which still contained half of a ham croquette and a dab of chicken salad.

"No, in the Bible God allows His people to eat flesh. I just don't hold with unnecessary killing. A snake shares this planet that God gave us. I respect other opinions, but that's how I feel."

"But what if you let a poisonous snake go, and it later attacks a child." When Ethel got a bit between her teeth, she was unstoppable.

"Aunt Ethel, I don't think—" Louise began, hoping to head off her challenge.

"That's a good point," Clay said, sounding as though he relished this kind of discussion. "The best way would be to trap the snake and take it to a wilderness area where it wouldn't be a danger to innocent people. But of course, not everyone is willing or able to do that."

"So your cousin did the right thing?" Ethel asked.

Clay smiled, accepting defeat graciously. "He reacted in self-defense. I wouldn't have wanted him to be bitten, especially not out running alone. But I think the more people get outside and understand how wondrous God's creation is, the less they'll be afraid of it."

"I'm still scared silly of snakes," Ethel insisted. "I guess it's a phobia, though, since I've never seen one in Acorn Hill. No reason to even think about them here."

"I'm glad to hear it, ma'am." Clay smiled broadly, showing a gleaming set of rather large teeth.

"Would you like another croquette, Clay?" Jane asked, passing the platter his way.

"If no one else wants it?" he asked, looking around the table.

No one spoke up except to encourage him to take the last one.

"I did have one real scare," he said between bites. "I was walking through farm country in Illinois, going south a ways to avoid the heavy traffic near Chicago. I'm used to dogs barking at me when I pass by. That's their job, guarding home turf. Most just make a lot of noise, then back off once I'm past their territory. Generally any dog will leave you alone if you're not afraid. They can always tell. Did you know they can smell a hundred times better than humans?"

"Were you attacked?" Ethel asked, rushing the story.

"Sort of. I was walking past this rundown farm. The house was probably a hundred years old and hadn't seen paint in half that time. The barn was tumbling down, and the only tractor in sight was a relic. My canteen was running low, and I needed to fill up, but I had a bad feeling about going up to that place. In fact, I thought it might be deserted, although there was a crop of corn on the surrounding acres. Sometimes the land gets bought or rented out, and the buildings are just left to tumble down. Cheaper than paying to have them wrecked and hauled away."

He paused to take a swallow of the iced tea that Jane had served with their meal.

"Then, just as I was passing a driveway partially overgrown with weeds, the baying started. I was speed walking, trying to act nonchalant but hoping to get beyond the edge of their territory. I was too slow, though. Before I knew it, I was up to my elbows in dogs, all of them mutts with only one thing in common—they were huge, and I thought for sure I was going to be mauled."

"Did they bite you?" Ethel asked breathlessly.

"Fortunately, no. One thing I know about dog packs is that you don't dare turn and run from them. Keeping as still as a statue, I shouted out orders for them to stay. Believe me, I was praying as hard as I could, and the Lord answered."

"The Lord stayed the wild beasts?" Ethel was clearly enthralled.

"Not exactly, but an old man came hobbling out of the decrepit house and shouted for them to come to him. They obeyed him instantly, just in time to save my hide. He shooed them away and apologized. He didn't think anyone would be walking along that road in the heat of day, and his dogs were only doing what came naturally. By way of making it up to me, he asked me up to the house, which was nicer inside than out. He and his wife must have been at least in their eighties, and, as I guessed, they rented the land instead of farming themselves anymore. None of his children or grandchildren was interested in the farm, so the old folks were living out their days alone.

"His wife had just baked a blueberry pie, so I had pie and iced tea with them. Once they learned I'd walked there from Nebraska, they couldn't hear enough about what I was doing. Ended up, I spent the night in their elder son's old room. It was like sleeping in a time capsule. They hadn't changed a thing since he left home for a career in the military in the sixties, but everything was spotless. They neglected the outside because it was too much for them to care for it, but everything inside was preserved like a museum. I think they enjoyed pretending I was one of theirs, just for one night."

"What a lovely story," Ethel said, her eyes looking a bit misty.

"The next day I stopped at a flower shop and had a nice mum plant delivered there because the wife missed being able to work in her garden. I warned the delivery person not to get out of the van until the dogs were called off," he said with a grin.

"Hello, is anyone home?" a voice trilled from the entryway.

"In here," Jane said, jumping up to greet the visitor.

"I didn't expect to interrupt your dinner. I thought you'd be done by now," Florence Simpson said, following her back to the dining room. "I stopped by to see Ethel—oh, there you are, Ethel. I thought you might be here since you weren't at home."

Alice took advantage of the interruption to begin clearing the table. No doubt Jane had a nice dessert in the kitchen, and everyone had enjoyed her informal dinner.

It wasn't surprising that Florence had come there looking for Ethel. At first glance, their gentle, sometimes girlish aunt, seemed to have little in common with her, but they shared an avid interest in everything that happened in Acorn Hill. As a longtime resident and one of the town's most prosperous citizens, Florence had a proprietary interest in all that went on, a characteristic that would have been annoying if it hadn't been tempered by her innate kindness.

To her credit, she had taken Ethel under her wing when their aunt first moved to Acorn Hill, and they remained close friends in spite of disagreements from time to time.

Tonight Florence's broad face was a bit flushed, her dark penciled eyebrows arching over watery gray eyes. Her hair was pulled back in a tight bun, a sure sign that she hadn't made her weekly visit to the beauty salon yet. She was wearing a crinkled-cotton blue and green print dress with short raglan sleeves that billowed around her stout figure. It was a cool choice for a hot August evening but an unusually casual garment for Florence, especially since she was wearing white sandals instead of her usual high heels.

Ethel quickly introduced her to Clay. "Clay walked here all the way from Nebraska," Ethel said, sounding as pleased as though he were her son. "Can you imagine, never once accepting a ride until Alice brought him here from Potterston Hospital? He's going to stay until his blisters heal."

Clay stood and took Florence's hand, smiling warmly and repeating her name.

"It's a pleasure to meet you, ma'am."

"All the way from Nebraska," Florence murmured.

It was as close to speechless as Alice had ever seen her.

"I'm embarrassed to admit that I drove here." Florence seemed flustered. "It's so hot tonight. Of course, usually I would have walked."

"Do sit down and join us for dessert," Jane said. "Clay has been telling us about some of his experiences along the way."

"Oh, I've had my supper. Well, maybe just a little taste. Who can resist one of your concoctions, Jane?" She sat opposite beside Clay, not noticing that Alice's water glass and napkin were still there.

"He narrowly avoided an attack by a dog pack," Ethel said with obvious pleasure in knowing something Florence didn't.

Alice smiled and finished clearing the table while Clay retold his stories with much prompting from Ethel. She'd never seen Florence listen to anyone with such rapt attention, and she had to admit that he was a spellbinder, even in the repetition of his narrative. She stopped clearing and stood with the empty salad bowl in her hands when he started telling about a trip he had made to Guatemala the previous year.

"The village was in the mountains, and nearly half the homes were destroyed by a mudslide. I was with a group rebuilding homes, striving to give some of the people sturdier houses in a safer location."

Clay was modest about his participation, but Jane could imagine him, surrounded by an adoring crowd of village children. Some aid workers distributed sweets or small toys to win the affection of the young, but she suspected that Clay's main gift was love.

"Now Clay is encouraging towns to build walking trails so more people get out and appreciate nature," Ethel said. "I've always said that children today spend far too much time watching television and playing with computers and such."

Alice couldn't remember her aunt ever saying that, but she marveled at Ethel's enthusiasm.

Jane hadn't planned on guests for dessert, but she came through with strawberry sundaes generously covered with freshly whipped cream. She served them in goblets with homemade ladyfingers. It was a dessert everyone liked, but Alice doubted whether any of the women at the table even noticed what they were eating. Clay was talking about summers spent with his grandparents in Georgia and what a wonderful example they were.

"I have my other grandmother to thank for making this trip possible with the legacy she left me. She lived with us when she got too old to live alone. I owe my love of nature to her. But my Georgia grandparents were the ones who taught me about service to others. When the bad hurricane hit New

Orleans, my grandmother worked at a soup kitchen, sleeping in their van because there wasn't any other place. Granddad worked on clearing debris until his bad back forced him to stop."

"I wonder if you'll be here long enough to talk to the people at Grace Chapel," Florence said. "Maybe you could speak after Sunday service. I imagine most of the congregation would stay, especially if I organize a potluck get-together. I'm sure Rev. Thompson would agree if I ask him."

"It would be my pleasure," Clay said after a brief pause, possibly to calculate how many days he might stay to let his blisters heal. "But I wouldn't want you to go to a lot of trouble on my account."

"Oh, it's no trouble at all," Florence said sounding thrilled. "I'll set up a calling committee to contact the members—after I get the okay from our minister, of course. It's always a good idea to assign different dishes so we don't end up with all desserts and no salads. My husband and I will order fried chicken from the market in Potterston. I think we'll be giving them enough notice. Ordinarily I'd fix it myself, but I'll be too busy setting up tables and arranging for nursery care for the young ones."

Ethel looked a bit deflated. She'd gone from being the-one-who-knew-the-walker to a mere onlooker as Florence planned a big event for him. No doubt it would be a sizable gathering, since Florence did have exceptional organizational skills. Sometimes, though, she forgot about people's feelings.

"That's a wonderful idea," Alice said. "I'm sure you and Ethel can get everything ready at short notice. You can be cochairs."

"I don't know—" Ethel began.

"Yes, we'll work together," Florence said as though it had been her idea.

"I think I have time this week," Ethel said, a rather weak attempt to show Florence that she was a busy person too.

"I want to thank the Lord and Ms. Jane for this bountiful meal," Clay said, bowing his head and taking Florence's and Ethel's hands in his much larger ones.

Alice smiled to herself as she bowed her head. She added peacemaker to Clay's many attributes.

Chapter Six

Alice never minded a panicked patient coming to the emergency room with a minor problem. She much preferred an overly cautious patient to one who waited until symptoms were disastrously severe, which was what happened Friday morning. She had to help Dr. Garcia with a stubborn middle-aged man who was trying to ignore a fever, nausea and a pain in the lower right portion of his abdomen.

"I have an important meeting this afternoon. You can schedule my surgery for tomorrow morning," Harold Kline insisted, sitting upright on the examining table. "I wouldn't be here if my secretary hadn't made such a fuss."

"Your secretary may have saved your life," Dr. Garcia said. "You have an elevated white blood cell count and acute inflammation of your appendix. If you delay the surgery, you risk peritonitis."

"All I need is a few hours. Then you can do your cutting." He attempted to smooth his salt-and-pepper hair, and he spoke with determination in his voice, trying to demonstrate that he could handle a little discomfort.

Alice was afraid the doctor was losing the argument. The patient was so fixated on his job that he wasn't letting the hospital do theirs. They couldn't force him to have immediate surgery, but Dr. Garcia had already called for a surgical team and reserved an operating room. Everything was ready except the permission form with Harold Kline's signature.

Fortunately, his secretary had called Mrs. Kline before driving her boss to the emergency room. His wife rushed into the examining cubicle just as the doctor was running out of arguments. Her sleekly styled blonde hair was held in place by lacquer, but she'd left home without makeup, wearing a pair of running shorts and a loose-fitting T-shirt, garb that attested to her urgent concern.

"What's going on?" she asked fearfully.

"Just a hot appendix," her husband said. "They can take care of it after my meeting with the Chambers group."

"Are you crazy? If that thing bursts, you could be history," she said, her voice growing shrill with worry. "Why is he sitting here? Shouldn't he be on his way to surgery?"

Dr. Garcia met her challenge calmly. "Everything is ready. All we need is his signature on this permission form."

"Give me that! I'll sign it. The man is mentally deranged." She seemed on the verge of tears.

"Calm down, you're making a scene," her husband said. "I'll sign it."

"I should think so! Your face is the color of day-old oatmeal."

Alice heaved a sigh of relief after she'd called attendants to wheel Mr. Kline away for surgery, his wife hurrying along beside him, still berating him for the delay. Alice said a prayer for his recovery, knowing he wouldn't be out of danger until after his appendix had been removed.

Dr. Garcia gave her a wan smile and went on to the next patient, a young teenager who had possibly broken a finger. His mother hovered over him, but he was taking it in stride, setting an example that some adults would do well to emulate.

Alice had had enough drama for one day, and it wasn't even time for her lunch break. This was promising to be a long day, and when her shift ended, she and Jody Monroe had an appointment with the woman who counseled diabetic patients on management of the disease. This interview would be for the lead article in the new wellness newsletter, and Alice was a little nervous about getting it right. She'd learned that every story had to have a hook, an idea to attract readers, and she'd started to make a list of questions as Carlene had suggested.

Jody would be writing it, but it was up to Alice to conduct the interview in a way that would give her the right kind of information. She had some questions jotted down in a small notebook, which would make it easy for her to read them over and add others while she ate her lunch.

That wasn't to be, though. As soon as she put her tray of salad and corn bread down on the table, Jody hurried over to join her.

"I was hoping I could catch you here," she said, sitting down across from Alice.

"Have you finished your lunch?" Alice asked.

"No, I brought one of those diet drinks instead. I'm trying to lose a little weight, but it's a struggle."

Alice couldn't fault her efforts, but she wasn't sure a can of liquid ingredients, however nutritious, was a good substitute for fresh fruit, vegetables and whole-wheat products.

"My mother thinks I'll have more self-confidence if I'm thinner," she confessed. "I won't be so intimidated by attractive people."

"You're lovely the way you are," Alice said kindly. "You have a very pretty face, and lots of girls would love to have your naturally curly hair. But losing a bit of weight *is* good for your health."

"I'm not exactly a poster child for wellness," Jody said unhappily, smoothing down the front of the bright pink cotton top she was wearing today. "Maybe I shouldn't be the one to write newsletter articles."

"Oh, please don't say that." Alice frowned. "I need you."

"Don't worry, I won't let you down. I only thought that I could sign your name to the articles. After all, you're doing the interviews, and people at the hospital respect you. I could be a ghostwriter."

"I won't hear of taking credit for your work," Alice assured her.

"I was afraid you might say that. Maybe I could use a pen name, you know, a pseudonym."

Alice shook her head. "This will be good for you. You'll get to know a lot more staff members."

"I can't think why they would want to know me," Jody said, half to herself.

Alice forgot about eating and interviewing. It made her sad to see a fellow professional and a sweet girl like Jody so down on herself.

"We're going to have fun with the newsletter," Alice assured her. "We'll get to know each other better, and you'll meet some new people. I'll see you at Trudy Chang's office after our shift."

"I got new batteries for my old tape recorder, so I guess we're ready to begin," she said with a worried expression on her face.

"It's been a madhouse today, so don't be concerned if I'm a few minutes late," Alice said. "I'll get there as soon as possible."

She wanted to suggest that Jody begin on her own, but maybe that would be pushing her too much.

Ethel had already dropped in on Jane once this morning, so her niece was surprised to see her again just before noon. This time she wasn't alone.

"Florence and I wanted to talk to Louise," she said from the kitchen door. "Do you know where she is?"

"We have something important to discuss with her," Florence said a bit mysteriously.

"She took Wendell to the vet for a checkup, but I expect her back any minute. Would you like a cup of tea while you wait?"

"Dear, it's unmercifully hot outside. Do you have any iced tea?" Ethel asked, fanning herself with an advertising brochure salvaged from her recycling bin.

"You're in luck. I made sun tea yesterday."

"I used to make sun tea," Florence said. "I have a huge glass jar. I like to put in around ten tea bags and let it sit in the sun to brew. It tastes so delicious, I can't think why I haven't done it this summer, but then, I do keep busy. My

Ronald requires a lot of looking after, and I seem to have accumulated so many responsibilities in the community."

"You can try my sun tea and see how it compares," Jane said, knowing that Florence would do exactly that—and let Jane know if it didn't meet her high standards.

She dropped ice cubes into two tall glasses and poured the amber-colored orange spice tea over it. What she didn't do was ask why they were eager to see Louise. Not that she wasn't curious, because both women seemed excited about something, but she would let them tell her in their own time.

Louise arrived home before they'd finished their tea— to which Florence gave high marks although she intimated that it didn't quite live up to hers. Louise came in the side door and set Wendell's carrier down with a relieved grunt, opening the door to set him free.

"I'm glad that's over with," she said, greeting Ethel and Florence as soon as she caught her breath from carrying the heavy load.

"Did Wendell get a good report from his checkup?" Jane asked, watching as their gray and black striped tabby scooted out of the hated cat carrier on his white-tipped paws.

He made a beeline for his feeding dish and, finding it empty, rubbed against her ankles.

"No treats for him!" Louise said before Jane could oblige their pet.

"Has he been a bad kitty?" Jane asked in surprise.

"Wendell has to go on a diet."

Jane's first impulse was to laugh, but she saw that her sister was serious.

"I have a printed sheet from the vet with suggestions, but our Wendell definitely needs to watch his figure."

"He's so fluffy it's hard to tell, but I guess maybe he has gained a little weight. I don't have the heart to deny him an occasional treat, though," Jane said.

"There's a solution for that. We're supposed to measure out his day's allowance of dry food, then feed him twice a day as usual. But we can save a little of the ration for treats. He won't feel deprived, but he'll be eating fewer calories."

"Will he lose weight that way?" Ethel asked.

"Yes, if he also exercises a little more."

"I don't think Wendell will take to being walked on a leash like a dog," Jane said.

"No," Louise said laughing. "We'll just have to make an effort to play with him more often. He loves games of chase. The vet said fifteen minutes a day could make a difference."

"Now that I think of it, he has been a bit sluggish lately. I thought it was natural because he's getting older," Jane said.

"According to the instruction sheet, most pets won't exercise on their own. I guess it's natural for them to conserve energy when there's no incentive to be active. Fortunately, our Wendell still loves to play. We can take turns thinking of ways to make physical activities fun for him."

"What else did the vet suggest?" Jane asked, taking the sheet Louise had pulled from her purse.

"Not to show love by overfeeding. Extra food isn't a good substitute for affection and playfulness. An important one is to keep pets away from the dinner table, but we usually do that anyway. Table treats are especially bad for a cat's health."

"Well, you certainly had a worthwhile trip to the vet," Florence said, signaling that she'd heard enough about Wendell's weight problem. "Ethel and I want to talk to you, Louise."

"I'll leave you here," Jane said. "I have a few things to do upstairs."

"Oh, you don't have to leave," her aunt said. "It's just that we don't think you need a fitness program. You're so slim and trim already—and, of course, you exercise on a regular basis."

"That's nice of you to say so, but I really do have some chores to do."

Jane excused herself and left with Wendell strolling after her.

"What are you two up to?" Louise asked Florence and her aunt, helping herself to a glass of sun tea.

"We have an idea," Ethel said, sounding a bit enigmatic.

"That wonderful young man, Clay, inspired it," Florence said enthusiastically. "By the way, how is he today? Do you think he'll be here long?"

"He was still limping at breakfast," Louise said. "It gives me shivers to think of walking on blisters, even after they've been drained. As for how long he'll stay, I don't think he knows himself. The doctor gave him strict orders to let his feet heal before resuming his trek. As it happens, we don't have bookings for all our rooms until later in the month, so he's a welcome guest for as long as he'd like to stay."

"He's so polite," Ethel said wistfully. "Did you see how he pulled out my chair at dinner? Not many young people are that thoughtful. And wasn't he interesting, talking about things that happened on his walk?"

"Yes, he seems very dedicated to his cause, but what is your idea?" Louise's first thought was that they wanted her to help with the potluck on Sunday. "Did Rev. Thompson agree to have a get-together after the service?"

"He not only agreed, he was really eager to meet Clay," Ethel said. "Florence and I went to the chapel first thing and were lucky enough to catch him before he left for a hospital visit."

"Then how can I help you?"

"We don't need help with the church brunch. I put the word out through my extensive network of friends, and Ethel will make more calls this afternoon," Florence said somewhat grandly. "We were so impressed with Clay that we've decided that we need to do more walking ourselves."

"We're fortunate that we don't really need a special trail. Acorn Hill is a lovely place to walk. There's so little traffic compared to bigger towns. And there are several quiet country roads right on the fringes of town," Ethel said.

"We're none of us as young as we were, and nothing is better for keeping fit than regular activity," Florence said. "But it's so tedious to exercise alone. I've tried using an exercise bike at home, but it's so boring that I can't force myself to do it every day."

"We've agreed—" her aunt began.

"Ethel and I, that is," Florence interrupted. "We're going to start an exercise group."

"Like a club. We'll take regular morning walks, then maybe gather for breakfast at the Coffee Shop."

"No pancakes or French toast for us, though," Ethel said. "We'll order healthy things like oatmeal or whole wheat toast."

Louise knew what was coming, and she tried to imagine squeezing a morning walk into her busy schedule.

"You're the first person we're asking to join us," Ethel said, making it sound like an honor.

"We'll start slowly at first, just a few blocks, then build up to longer walks," Florence said. "We'll leave early in the morning while it's still cool. We know that you give most of your lessons in the afternoon, so you're the perfect person to join us."

"We're going to ask others too," her aunt said. "Imagine how much fun it will be to have a whole parade of people out for a bracing morning walk."

"We agreed that I would be the first president," Florence said.

"Why do you need one?" Louise asked in surprise.

"Oh, you know, to encourage everyone not to miss any mornings and to recruit new members. Maybe I'll plan a special outing from time to time, like driving to an especially nice place. I can imagine all of us strolling through the woods when the leaves have turned in the fall. Or going to the mall in Potterston once it gets too cold."

"We thought five mornings a week would be enough. There wouldn't be time before services on Sunday," Ethel noted.

"And so many people like to go to Potterston to shop on Saturday," Florence said.

"I'm going to be the secretary and keep a log of how far we walk every morning. I've heard that you can buy a pedometer, a little gadget that attaches to a waistband or belt and measures distance. Maybe Fred has them at his hardware store," Ethel said.

"If not, I'm sure I can find one in Potterston," Florence said.

Louise felt bowled over by their enthusiasm, but she recognized the merit of their idea. She made a special point of walking often, but she had serious doubts about keeping to their schedule. One of the great things about walking for exercise was that it could be done any time, alone or with someone.

"It's a wonderful idea, but I'm not sure I could join you every morning. Some days my schedule is pretty full, and when Alice is working, I help Jane with the guests' breakfast by setting and clearing the table."

"You can't do that!" Florence said emphatically.

"It's not fair to make Jane do all the work," Louise said defensively.

"That's not what I mean. The first rule of our walking club is not to make excuses. You need exercise every day, not just the times when you're not doing anything else." Florence was beginning to sound like a drill sergeant.

They have two members, and already they have rules, Louise thought. This was beginning to sound like a typical Florence project.

"We won't be starting that early," Ethel assured her in a gentle tone. "Florence has to fix Ronald's breakfast first, and neither of us is what you call an early bird. We thought a nine o'clock start would be reasonable."

"When do you plan to begin?" Louise asked, sensing that they weren't going to take no for an answer.

"Monday," they said in unison.

"We're going to meet in front of Grace Chapel promptly at nine," Ethel said.

"We thought that was a good starting place," Florence said. "It's close for you and Ethel, and those of us who live farther away can drive and park there."

"I'm not making any promises," Louise said. "Some days it just won't work for me."

"We understand how busy you are with the inn and your lessons," Ethel said. "But it would mean so much if you would join us whenever you can. After all, you're my niece, and I care about your health. It's never too late to pay more attention to physical fitness."

"We're going to Potterston this afternoon to get some sensible walking shoes," Florence said. "With my bunion, I need to be fitted by an expert."

"We thought we would celebrate our new group by having lunch at the Knife and Fork," Ethel said. "They have such a lovely noon buffet."

"In fact, we'd better get going so it won't be all picked over when we get there. You're welcome to join us."

Louise thanked them for the invitation but declined, using her students' lessons as an excuse. It boggled her mind to celebrate the beginning of an exercise program with a big lunch, but a walking group wasn't a bad idea. Ethel and Florence would benefit, and they might recruit a number of other people who rarely got out to exercise. She wished them well in spite of her own reservations about joining them.

Alice couldn't believe it, but she was actually a little nervous about her first interview. She knew the diabetes educator casually, but using her as the subject of an article was quite different from saying hello in the corridor.

Trudy Chang had taken the job at the hospital about three years ago when her husband took over management of the recycling plant between Potterston and Acorn Hill. They were both Asian-Americans who traced their ancestry back to the Chinese work gangs who built western rail lines in the 1800s. They called San Francisco home, but they'd been lured to Pennsylvania by the challenge of expanding the area's recycling efforts. Alice felt the community was very fortunate to have them, and she'd heard excellent things about Trudy's work with diabetes patients.

Jody was waiting for her outside Trudy's office. She'd changed out of her nurse's uniform and was wearing denim pants and a pale blue cotton knit tank top. If she'd put on street clothes to boost her confidence, it didn't seem to be working. She was pacing back and forth in front of the closed office door, looking so agitated that Alice forgot about her own momentary bout of nervousness.

"This will be fun," Alice whispered. "Mrs. Chang is a lovely person. She'll want to spread the word about ways to prevent diabetes."

Alice wished that she had more questions jotted down in her notebook, but it was too late to think of additional ones.

"Just so long as I don't have to do the talking," Jody said. "I'm not good at meeting new people."

"You meet new people, your patients, every day," Alice reminded her.

"Yes, but I know what to do with them. It's my job to see that they're comfortable and well cared for. I suspect that they only see my uniform anyway."

There wasn't time to give Jody more encouragement. They were nearly five minutes late as it was. She knocked softly on the door, and it was opened immediately by the slender, dark-haired diabetes educator.

Trudy Chang had opted not to wear a uniform when she met her patients, dressing today in a buttercup-yellow linen summer suit with a silky lavender blouse. Her office was as welcoming as any in the hospital with a grouping of comfortable ebony chairs around a low table. Books shared space on the shelves with a collection of brass, ceramic and glass pandas, and she'd covered the walls with stylized floral prints.

"I'm so excited to do this," she said, motioning them to sit at the table where she'd laid a plate of cinnamon rice cakes, a teapot and tiny porcelain cups.

"It's Red Zinger," she said indicating the tea. "May I pour some for you?"

"I'd love a cup," Alice said. "Trudy, this is Jody Monroe. She'll be recording our interview, with your permission, and writing it up for the newsletter."

"It's a pleasure to meet you, Jody. Of course, you can tape. I admire anyone who can write. I agonize when I have to write anything, even a letter to a friend. Please, have one of my rice cakes. I buy plain ones, then glaze them with my own special sugar-free cinnamon topping."

Alice tried one and pronounced it delicious, but Jody appeared frozen in place. It seemed best to get on with the interview and hope her helper relaxed as they went along.

"Where shall we begin?" Trudy asked. "I have to admit, I'm a bit nervous. I would hate to say something that gives the wrong impression of what I try to do. People tease me in the lunchroom if I'm eating anything but salad. I'm afraid I come across as something of a crusader, but I see so many people whose lifestyle has been drastically altered by diabetes."

"You will do fine, I'm sure. Now, my first question is, can diabetes be prevented?" Alice asked, knowing that she had to get down to basics so Jody would have good material for the article.

"Yes, in many cases type 2 diabetes can be prevented, or at least put off. Are you going to limit the article to what used to be called adult-onset diabetes?"

"Since we're confined to five hundred to seven hundred words, that would probably be best." Alice was beginning to get the feel for a hook. "We're writing for health-care professionals, so I don't think we need to discuss childhood diabetes in the same article. Maybe the main emphasis would be ways to prevent type 2."

"Then let's focus on people who are prediabetic. That would be anyone whose blood glucose is higher than normal but below the diabetes range. They're the ones most at risk for getting type 2 and heart disease, which is closely associated with diabetes. Being diabetic means that the body doesn't make and use insulin properly. Left untreated, a severe case can even cause blindness and require amputations, but I wouldn't want your article to resort to scare tactics."

"No, we definitely want to be positive," Alice said.

"Maybe the article should encourage everyone to have blood tests," Jody said.

"Good idea." Alice was glad that her helper had decided to participate in the interview.

"I have some literature for you. It includes the notebook I give patients. The main thing I want to emphasize is that prediabetics can experience a return to normal blood glucose levels with modest weight loss and moderate physical exercise," Trudy said. "A reasonable goal is to lose five to seven percent of body weight."

"That doesn't sound like an awful lot," Jody quietly commented.

"I always stress setting reasonable goals. Losing one pound a week and keeping it off is better than a crash diet that is soon reversed."

"It's not as easy as it sounds, though," the young nurse said.

Alice mentally scrapped her list of questions. Jody's genuine concern was bringing out exactly what was needed for the article.

"The first thing I recommend is exercising at least thirty minutes a day. Some people like group activities such as aerobics or a health club, but the simplest is a brisk walk. It costs nothing but time and is available to everyone. In bad weather, our local mall opens the door for walkers at 6:00 AM. I've gone there myself, and there are always a number of people taking advantage of it."

"I imagine it takes careful planning to find thirty minutes in a person's busy schedule," Alice said.

"Yes, but it's the most important half hour of the day. The most rewarding too. Not only does it help prevent diabetes, it gives a person more energy for other tasks."

"I walk with my mother almost every evening, but I don't seem to lose weight from it," Jody said.

"Then it's time to take a hard look at your daily diet. First you have to make wise food choices. I recommend substituting vegetables and fruits in place of high-carb choices, but I don't think extreme changes work well. Eat a balanced diet, taking care not to include too much sodium or excessive carbohydrates."

"I try to do that," Jody said.

"The other thing to watch is the size of your portions. You don't have to weigh and measure everything—mainly because it's tedious and few stick with it. But limit the amount you eat. For example, your meat, poultry or fish serving should be no larger than a deck of playing cards. Half a baked potato should satisfy as well as a whole, or better still, substitute a nutrient-rich sweet potato. Fill the empty space in your tummy with green and yellow vegetables."

Trudy laughed at herself. "I could go on about diet all day, but you'll find lots of help in the notebook I'm giving you."

"Knowing what to do and doing it are two different things," Alice said.

"How well I know," Trudy responded. "I urge my patients to make a plan and follow it. Some like to make a weight chart and check off their losses. Others work out a menu for the week and buy only the foods that belong on it. Hardly anyone will go out late at night to buy ice cream, but most of us can be tempted if the freezer is well stocked with it. The first step toward weight loss has to be wise shopping."

"Not everyone lives alone," Jody said. "Others might not appreciate restrictive shopping."

"It helps immensely if you live with people who are understanding and supportive," Trudy said, "but you have to take a firm stand and insist on eating a healthy diet."

"My mother says that I should lose weight, but she cooks too much food, especially when my dad is home from his job with the railroad. She hates to see things go to waste."

"So she urges you to be her human disposal," Trudy said sympathetically.

"Well, she's not that bad, but I was brought up to clean my plate. It doesn't feel right to waste food, even if she doesn't say anything."

"There's a difference between getting children to eat what's good for them and insisting they eat everything that's put in front of them. Nothing is harder than breaking a longtime habit. That's why I'm excited to emphasize this in your article. If it were easy, all prediabetics could do it on their own with no outside support. And here's another major point—find a support group."

"Do you mean a weight-loss group? I've heard they can be expensive," Jody said.

"That's an option, but I was thinking of a few friends or family members who are sympathetic, perhaps people who have the same concerns and need to work on improving their own diet and exercise program."

"I have a friend from high school who had a baby last year. She's having a terrible time getting her weight back down," Jody said.

"There, you have the beginning of a support group. Maybe you could exercise together or share ideas for meals."

"I think I'll give her a call tonight and see how she's doing," Jody said thoughtfully.

"I also suggest rewarding yourself for success, say every time you lose a certain number of pounds or reach an exercise goal. But never, never use food as a reward. Instead treat yourself to something else you really like: a movie, a spa visit, a new pair of shoes."

"The biggest reward might be feeling better about yourself," Jody said.

"That and decreasing the chance of type 2 diabetes," Alice said, immensely pleased that Jody was participating so fully in the discussion.

They talked awhile longer, none of them eager to end such an inspiring interview. Finally Alice and Jody thanked Trudy for her time and all the valuable information, then walked to the parking lot together.

"You were wrong, you know," Alice said.

"Did I do something I shouldn't have?" Jody asked in surprise.

"Absolutely not. You were wrong in believing that you couldn't do an interview. You did a marvelous job asking the right questions."

"Mrs. Chang was so pleasant and eager to share her knowledge. I couldn't help being interested. I hope you don't mind that I talked so much."

"I'm delighted with your assistance," Alice assured her, deciding that their first interview couldn't have been more successful.

Chapter Seven

*T*ell me, is this your first stay at Grace Chapel Inn?"
Vern Snyper asked Mr. and Mrs. Comstock, the couple
who sat across from him and his wife at breakfast Saturday
morning.

Louise paused in the doorway, holding a basket of freshly
baked biscuits she was bringing to the table.

"Oh my, no," Mrs. Comstock said. "We stay here whenever we travel to Cleveland to visit our daughter's family.
She has two sons and a daughter, all under school age."

"We like to rest up a bit on the way there and home," her
husband added. "We're crazy about our grandkids, but they
wear us out. The oldest, Tommy, waits for me on the front
porch with his ball. Don't tell me kids have short attention
spans. He'd have me playing catch with him from dawn to
dark if I were up to it."

"You're exaggerating," his wife playfully rebuked him.

"How did you hear about this place?" Isabel Snyper
asked. "I've never seen their advertising in any travel
magazines."

"Good thing," Mr. Comstock said. "If too many people learned about what a great stopping place this is, we wouldn't be able to get reservations."

"Actually, a friend of ours told us about it," his wife said. "She raved so much about the Victorian house and the wonderful hospitality that we had to try it ourselves."

"So word of mouth is important," Vern said more to himself than the others at the table.

"Have you stayed at other bed-and-breakfasts?" Isabel asked.

"A few," Mrs. Comstock said. "Especially when we did a color tour of New England last fall."

"How does this one compare?" Isabel pressed.

"It's our home away from home," Mr. Comstock answered. "Say, why don't we have fresh-squeezed juice like this at home, honey?"

"Because you never get up in time to fix it," his wife teased.

Louise was still puzzled by the kinds of probing questions asked by the Snypers, but she moved quietly to the table and put down the biscuits.

"What's the main course?" Mr. Comstock asked. "This is the only time I get real eggs."

"Then you won't be disappointed," Louise said. "Jane's Spanish-style cheese soufflé will be ready in a minute."

"That means you shouldn't fill up on biscuits," Mrs. Comstock warned her husband, whose plump, good-natured face and full white beard reminded Louise of a department store Santa's.

"You can bet I have room for both," he said grinning.

Louise headed back to the kitchen, but she could still hear Vern quizzing the other couple.

"Do you get a discount as a frequent guest?" he asked.

"Certainly not." Mrs. Comstock sounded offended by the suggestion. "I'm sure the Howard sisters treat all their guests the same."

"Equally well," her husband added.

"They're doing it again," Louise, out in the kitchen, whispered to her sister.

"Who's doing what?" Jane was intent on gingerly taking the soufflé from the oven.

"The Snypers are asking all kinds of questions."

"Maybe they're just making conversation."

"By asking whether Mr. and Mrs. Comstock get a discount as frequent guests?"

"That's cheeky, but I don't know what we can do about it," Jane agreed, preparing to take her soufflé to the table and serve it herself. "Have you seen Clay this morning? He wasn't down for breakfast when I last checked the dining room."

"No, the poor boy must be exhausted after his journey. Alice inspected his feet yesterday and isn't very happy about the infection. She even suggested taking him back to see Dr. Garcia again, but he didn't feel quite ready for that. He said that when the Lord wanted him to walk again, his feet would be healed."

"He has amazing faith," Jane said. "I'd better serve the soufflé now. I won't save any for Clay. I can make something fresh when he comes down."

Alice was enjoying an early morning outing with her walking partner, Vera Humbert. Although Vera was ten years younger, her friendship with Alice went back many years to the time when she'd become engaged to her husband Fred, owner of the local hardware store. Vera fought her tendency to be slightly plump by walking whenever she could, although it was not easy for the two women to walk together during the school year. Vera taught fifth grade at Acorn Hill Elementary School. This, combined with Alice's shift changes at the hospital, made it difficult to get out at the same time, but they made it a priority to walk every Saturday.

After they exchanged family news, the conversation drifted to Vera's plans for the next school year and Alice's new project at the hospital, the wellness newsletter.

"I didn't know you like to write," Vera said, a bit surprised by Alice's new job.

"I don't, but I have a lovely young nurse who's volunteered to help. In fact, I should speak to Jane. It would be nice to have her for a meal sometime soon, especially since we have an interesting guest around her age. We could invite both of them for Sunday supper."

"Who is this guest?"

"A young man who's walking from Nebraska to New York to promote hiking and biking trails. He's been slowed by infected blisters, so he's staying with us until they heal. You and Fred might enjoy meeting him too. I'll speak to Jane, and if she has time for a dinner party, I'll let you know. If you'd like to come, that is."

"We would be delighted. You know Fred, he loves to talk to new people."

The more Alice thought about it, the more inspired her idea seemed. Clay must be getting restless from his enforced break, and Jody needed practice meeting new people. With Vera and Fred at the meal too, it was sure to be a lively event.

⌒

Louise helped clear the table and load the dishwasher, and then went to the inn's library. The sign on the door said the Daniel Howard Library. Louise sometimes did her accounting and bill paying at his desk, finding the ambiance of the room perfect for quiet concentration. The walls were papered in a mossy green tweed that complemented the mahogany furnishings. The rust, gold and black Oriental rug and russet-colored chairs made the room handsome, and the many personal touches made it inviting. Framed family photos were hung behind the desk, and the best examples from his pen collection were kept on display in a mahogany box.

Since it was only the ninth of August, no new bills had accumulated, but Louise had recently learned about some handles that could be attached with suction to make entering or exiting a tub or shower safer. She'd talked it over with her sisters, and they'd decided to order one for each guest bathroom. If they worked as promised, then they would buy more for their own safety.

She was thumbing through the mail-order catalog to find the right page when there was a soft knock on the library door.

"Come in," Louise called out.

"I do hope I'm not disturbing you," Isabel Snyper said. "I wanted to tell you what a lovely breakfast it was."

"I'm glad you enjoyed it, but Jane deserves the credit."

"I imagine much of the success of your bed-and-breakfast depends on her wonderful cooking." Isabel sat down on the russet chair closest to the desk and settled back.

She was looking a bit perkier this morning. Instead of her usual formal outfit, she was wearing a blue, woven cotton dress that buttoned down the front. Her salt-and-pepper hair looked recently styled, so perhaps she'd taken advantage of her vacation time to visit a salon. But what else did she do to occupy herself all day? That was what Louise wanted to know but was too polite to ask.

"I'm sure her breakfasts contribute a lot to our success. We're fortunate that she's a professional chef," Louise said, again wondering why Isabel asked so many questions.

"What part of your budget goes to food?" she asked in a casual tone.

"We've never figured it exactly." Louise wasn't usually evasive, but the question was one that would require some computation.

"You must have a ballpark idea," Isabel persisted.

Louise struggled with her conscience before answering. She'd never been rude to a guest under any circumstances, but the Snypers were asking questions about matters that were really none of their concern. Discussing the inn's finances went way beyond the bounds of courtesy.

She shook her head and asked a question of her own.

"Is there some special reason why you want to know?"

"Oh, just curious," Isabel said, shrugging her shoulders and smiling.

"Are you sure that's all there is to it?" Louise asked in a mild voice, looking directly into the guest's partly hooded dark brown eyes.

"I told Vern that you'd find us out eventually," she said, sounding as guilty as a child caught snitching cookies. "We do have an ulterior motive."

Louise didn't say anything, letting her silent scrutiny indicate that she wanted to hear the whole truth.

"We're seriously thinking of retiring," Isabel said, nervously bunching a handful of her full skirt in her fist. "Vern has done well in his investments, and I have a good client list for my decorating business. But we're not getting any younger. We want to change our lifestyle, but lying around on a beach doesn't appeal to either of us. We'll need something to occupy us if we leave our present occupations."

"And?" Louise gently encouraged her.

"I've always wanted to try running a bed-and-breakfast. Vern is agreeable to the idea, but we wanted to investigate a few good ones before we make our final decision."

"I see."

"Your inn has a wonderful reputation. We had friends stay here once, and they raved about it. So naturally, we thought this would be a good place to begin our research."

"Grace Chapel Inn isn't for sale," Louise firmly informed her, wanting to squelch any offer they might make.

"No, we didn't expect that it would be. We were just hoping to get some idea of what makes a bed-and-breakfast successful. Naturally we want ours to be a financial success if we decide to go ahead with it. You ladies seem to be thriving, so we're curious about your management techniques. There's something special going on here, and we can't quite put our fingers on it."

"I can give you a simple answer to that," Louise said. "It's a labor of love. We grew up in this house and feel privileged to be able to live here together. Our guests are important to us, and not just as a source of income."

"But you must be getting good returns since three of you are making a living here."

Louise felt that Isabel had again crossed a line. She didn't intend to explain the family's financial situation to a stranger. Her husband had left her reasonably comfortable, and she augmented her personal spending money by giving piano lessons. Alice still worked at the hospital, and she would have a nice pension when she retired for good. Jane was largely dependent on the inn's revenue, but she had been careful about saving, and she'd invested wisely. Louise and Alice were both eligible for social security, although her sister hadn't yet applied.

"Or perhaps it's more of a hobby with you," Isabel speculated.

"Not at all," Louise said truthfully. "It's no small expense to keep a large Victorian home in good order."

"So perhaps a bed-and-breakfast would be more profitable if the house was newer," she said.

"I wouldn't know about that."

"Well, I've taken enough of your time," Isabel said, standing to leave. "Thank you for being such a gracious hostess."

"You're welcome."

Louise hoped that this was the last of Isabel and Vern's prying. At least she now knew that they were more than exceptionally curious guests.

"Good morning," Clay said limping into the kitchen. "I'm afraid I missed breakfast."

"Not at all," Jane assured him. "Our breakfast hours are only suggested times. I won't hear of a guest going hungry."

"I don't want to put you to a lot of trouble," he said, looking around the kitchen. "A bowl of cereal would do me fine."

"I made soufflés for the other guests. It wouldn't be any trouble at all to whip one up for you."

"Eggs would be nice," he said grinning sheepishly, his fair complexion less ruddy after some time away from the open road. "Maybe scrambled."

"How about an omelet?" Jane asked. "I can put in cheese, bacon, green and red peppers, onions, mushrooms —oh, and I have some frozen hash browns that work pretty well with omelets. What's your pleasure, Perry Clay Garfield?"

"All that would be great," he said smiling broadly. "If I don't get back to walking soon, I'm going to be a blimp. I've been having lunch and dinner at the Coffee Shop, and they really serve a full plate. Not as tasty as your breakfasts," he was quick to add, "but good."

"Any trouble walking over there?" she asked.

Jane had already offered to drive him anywhere he wanted to go, as had Alice, but he insisted that he had to go on his own steam.

"No, I'm getting along fine. You've been so nice to me already that I hate to ask, but would it be all right if I do a load of laundry here? I haven't seen a Laundromat."

"Of course. I can throw things in the washing machine for you, if you like."

"No, I can do it," he assured her. "I've been doing my own laundry for years."

Jane smiled at his self-reliance, but then, what else could she expect from a young man who was crossing half the country alone and on foot? She poured a big glass of fresh orange juice and set about making him a king-size omelet.

Alice came back from her walk just as Clay was finishing the omelet and a stack of buttered toast made from Jane's homemade German caraway bread. Her face was pink from the morning heat, and she sank down gratefully on a chair opposite their guest, sipping the glass of ice water Jane put in front of her.

"You and Vera must have had a long walk," Jane said after Alice exchanged greetings with Clay.

"I felt as if we were headed to Nebraska," Alice joked. "It's that hot out. I don't know how you handle the heat walking across the plains states, Clay."

"With lots of sunscreen, dark-tinted goggles, long sleeves, a bandanna around my neck and my cowboy hat. People laugh at it in this part of the country, but it's a good sun shade. And water, lots of water. Dehydration is a distance walker's greatest enemy. I start off every morning with a heavy load and end the day with all my bottles empty."

"Good advice," Alice said. "I carry one bottle, but on a day like this, I should have more. But I did have a good idea while we were walking."

"What?" Jane asked.

"I thought maybe we could have a cookout this Sunday."

"Sounds good, but have you forgotten Florence and Ethel's brunch after church?"

"No, I thought we could have it in the evening once it starts to cool off a bit. The days are still pretty long, so we could plan it for seven and it will still be light. That is, if you're willing," she said to her sister.

"I'd love it. I've been wanting to try a new barbecue sauce. I found the recipe online, and it calls for some ingredients I've never used in mine."

"I thought we could ask Vera and Fred," Alice said. "And Aunt Ethel, of course."

"Would you like to join us old folks Sunday evening?" Jane asked Clay.

"You'd be doing me a big favor," Alice said. "One of the younger nurses at the hospital has been helping me with the wellness newsletter, and I'd love to thank her by including her in the cookout. I'm sure she would enjoy it more if there was someone closer to her own age."

"I'd be happy to join you if you're not tired of feeding me," Clay said, finishing off the refill of orange juice Jane had just poured for him. "I talked to a man named Fred in the hardware store. I was hoping to replace a leaky water bottle with a new one designed for hikers, and sure enough, he had one."

"That's our Fred," Alice said. "His hardware store is a lifesaver. I never cease to marvel at how many different useful things he has in stock."

"He's been studying the weather," Clay said. "He predicts the hot, dry spell will last until mid-September."

"Fred is quite an amateur weather prognosticator," Alice said. "If he says rain, Vera and I carry our umbrellas."

"He had some interesting things to say about global warming," Clay said in an animated voice. "He's been watching what the Japanese have been doing to save Tokyo from catastrophic floods. They have a system of huge underground tanks to contain the water. He recorded a cable program about them and invited me to come see it at his house sometime."

"Then you're going to have a lot to discuss with him at the cookout," Alice said with satisfaction, although she hoped he and Jody would find some common ground too.

It might do her young friend a world of good to get to know Clay. While she mentioned girlfriends from time to time, she was painfully shy with men, even the hospital's interns who tended to be close to her age and quite gregarious. Alice didn't approve of matchmaking, but her conscience was clear this time. There was no question that Clay would soon resume his walk, so this would only be a casual meeting—that is, if Jody agreed to come.

Clay finished his breakfast and left after a bit, and Alice used the kitchen phone to issue her invitations. Jody, Vera and Fred accepted, but Ethel wasn't answering her phone. Alice hung up just as Louise came into the kitchen.

"Well, I have some news about our inquisitive guests," she said in a low voice.

Jane and Alice came closer to hear her, knowing it was possible that their normal voices could be heard by guests in the foyer.

"I knew they weren't just ordinary guests," Louise said. "You know how they keep asking questions, and we never know where they'll turn up."

"Even in the attic," Alice reminded her.

"Well, they do have an ulterior motive. They're thinking of starting a bed-and-breakfast of their own. They're here to learn all they can about the way we do things."

She explained how Isabel had come to her to ask about food expenses.

"I would feel better about this if they had been up-front about it," Jane said thoughtfully. "They've been acting like—"

"Spies," Alice said emphatically.

Ethel came into the kitchen just in time to hear the last word.

"What about spies?" she asked excitedly.

"I was just dramatizing," Alice said, not wanting to involve their aunt.

"Well, do I have news for you," Ethel said. "You know that Florence is friends with Cornelia Black, the real estate agent who's in business with her husband. They handle mostly farm properties and acreages, but Cornelia let slip that she has a couple interested in the Bigelow house."

"I know that name, but I can't place where the house is," Jane said.

"It's that huge modern house on the outskirts of town. Everyone was surprised when they built it. Why would anyone erect such a palace so close to Acorn Hill? Anyway, it turned out to be unlucky," Ethel said. "The owners divorced and moved away, and the house has been on the market for ages. It's just too large and pretentious for our little town, I suppose."

Alice had learned long ago to let her aunt's gossip go in one ear and out the other, especially when Florence was the source. Not that the two of them didn't have a handle on all that happened in the town, but Alice didn't like to encourage Ethel's fascination with rumors and half-truths. This time, though, something about her news hit home.

"Did Florence learn anything about the people who are interested in buying it?" she asked.

Louise said what Alice was thinking. "Could it be our guests, the Snypers?"

"All Cornelia said was that they were from New Jersey. They asked her to check on the zoning and such, so they must be serious about making an offer. I suspect the property will go quite reasonably since it's been on the market such a long time."

"The Snypers must be thinking of starting another bed-and-breakfast there," Louise said. "It's an ideal location if you think about it, with lots of room for parking and other features."

"It already has a swimming pool in back," Ethel said.

"The nerve!" Jane said. "Spying on our operation when they're scheming to become our competition. We should ask them to leave."

"Oh dear." Alice winced. "I don't think we can do that."

Louise frowned. "They've abused our hospitality, but I don't know whether we can withdraw it. Let's not make any hasty decisions."

"You're probably right," Jane agreed, sounding reluctant. "It's not what Grace Chapel Inn is all about. But I don't know whether two bed-and-breakfasts can survive in a town as small as Acorn Hill."

"They would have an advantage being closer to the interstate," Alice said.

"This could be really bad for you, couldn't it?" Ethel asked, her faced creased with worry.

"Unfortunately, yes," Jane said. "But don't fret, Aunt Ethel. They haven't bought it yet, and we don't know for sure that it would ruin our business. Some of our guests are quite loyal."

"We might have to put in another guest bathroom to compete," Louise said. "That could be terribly expensive, but people do like private baths."

"I'm so annoyed," Jane admitted. "They've been poking their noses into everything we do, asking dozens of questions about how we manage things."

"It distresses me that they've also been questioning our guests," Louise said. "I'm not sure I can endure so many days of their intrusion."

"Five days, if I remember right. I can check the book," Jane said.

"Our hospitality is certainly being tested," Alice said. "Maybe we'll have to grit our teeth and be professional about this."

"Let's give it some thought," Louise suggested. "I feel that I need to pray about it before I can decide."

"Yes," Alice agreed. "I don't feel ready to make a hasty decision. It would be nice if they have the grace to leave on their own. Maybe if we confront them with what we know, they'll want to leave."

"Sensitivity doesn't seem to be their strong point," Jane said. "I don't think we can count on that."

"Dear, I feel as though I've stirred up a hornet's nest," Ethel said. "Maybe I shouldn't have said anything."

"Don't think that," Alice said. "If it's true, then we needed to know."

"Oh, it is," Ethel said. "Florence and I do like a bit of gossip on occasion, I'm afraid, but Cornelia said they've looked at the Bigelow house three times. That sounds like they're seriously considering an offer to buy."

"Let's make our decision this evening," Louise said. "I suggest we meet in the library after dinner. Meanwhile, I should lock that door. With their track record, it might be that the Snypers will want to look for our financial records."

Not long afterward, Louise went up to her room with a heavy heart. They'd had a few guests who were annoying, but many more were lovely people. She felt that her life had been enriched by meeting such a diverse group, but this was the first time she'd felt betrayed. Isabel and

Vern Snyper had operated under false pretenses. If they'd told the sisters about their intentions, she wouldn't feel so offended.

What had they been doing in the quiet hours when no one was observing them?

This wasn't like a guest stealing a towel, something that rarely happened at Grace Chapel Inn. The Snypers wanted to run a newer, more conveniently located bed-and-breakfast. Louise had serious doubts whether Acorn Hill could support two.

In the quiet of her room, Louise knelt beside her bed in prayer, asking the Lord for the wisdom to know what to do and the strength to do it.

She felt calmer, but she still didn't know about asking the Snypers to leave. Her Bible was lying in its accustomed place, the dark red cover scuffed from constant use and the spine beginning to weaken. She'd thought several times of buying a new one, but she was deeply attached to this one. The word of the Lord as found in her familiar copy had seen her through many times of sorrow and indecision, especially after her dear husband had passed on. Surely she could find words of guidance for this lesser crisis.

It wasn't her usual way to flip the pages and put her finger on a random passage, hoping fate would lead her to the right answer. Instead she relied on her familiarity with the books of the Bible to find a source of inspiration.

Today Louise felt drawn to Galatians, a letter Paul had written to the church in Galatia to strengthen their faith in the gospel of Christ. She began reading the first chapter, but not until she reached the sixth and last one did she find a passage that helped clear her mind:

"Let us not become weary in doing good, for at the proper time we will reap a harvest if we do not give up" (Galatians 6:9).

Sometimes doing good is uncommonly difficult, Louise thought, *but the Lord never promised that following Him would be easy. Perhaps the hardest of all the rules Jesus laid down for His followers was to love one's enemy.*

Dinner was a quiet meal. Jane chatted a bit about her menu plan for the cookout, but Alice knew that there was one pressing concern on all their minds. She'd made her decision, but she didn't want to say anything until they gathered in the library as they had agreed.

They did so immediately after eating, leaving their dishes on the kitchen table by unspoken consent.

"Well," Jane said when they met behind the closed door of the library. "What are we going to do about the Snypers?

I have to admit that I am deeply concerned about the possibility of being forced out by competition. I can't imagine going back to restaurant work after the wonderful times I've had here."

"It's harder on you," Alice agreed. "You're a long way from being old enough to retire, not that Louise and I have any desire to do so."

"Yes," Jane agreed, "but I want to do what's right. I feel very conflicted."

"If we look at this as a way of keeping the faith, our decision becomes easier," Alice said in a loving way, understanding why Jane didn't feel she could continue offering hospitality to the Snypers.

"I read a Bible passage that seemed to speak to me," Louise said, quoting from memory the verse from Galatians that had steadied her. "The Lord never gives us a difficult task without the promise of a reward. Perhaps the Snypers do have the means to put us out of business, but we've been greatly blessed in so many ways. I don't want to compromise our principles because they've taken advantage of us."

"I agree," Alice said.

"Yes, I guess I do too," Jane said. "If loving our enemies were easy, the Lord wouldn't have urged us to recognize how important it is."

"We're agreed then," Alice said. "The Snypers can stay for the time they reserved, but I think we should let them know what we've learned about their plans."

"Then if they feel uncomfortable, they can cancel their reservation without any financial penalty," Louise said. "I'll take it upon myself to speak to them."

"And keep the library door locked," Jane said. Then she giggled in spite of herself.

Chapter Eight

*A*lice stayed behind to wait for Clay after her sisters had left early for church. Louise would be playing the organ, and Ethel had recruited Jane to do a few jobs before the service to get ready for the brunch. She especially needed her help with the big coffeemaker, since it was something of a puzzle to their aunt.

Their guest didn't keep Alice waiting. He announced that he was looking forward to services, but he added apologetically, "I didn't bring any good clothes for church. I hope I won't embarrass you."

"Not at all. You look fine," Alice said.

She was impressed that he'd laundered his clothes and borrowed Jane's iron to press one of his better pairs of jeans. His long-sleeved light blue knit shirt wasn't exactly formal wear, but it was perfectly acceptable. Some members of the congregation dressed to the nines, notably Florence and a few of the older women, but Rev. Kenneth Thompson had let it be known that there was no dress code. He much preferred casual wear to a competitive fashion parade every Sunday.

Alice was wearing a lightweight two-piece print dress in shades of blue. The hem was fashionably long, making it a nice change from her uniforms and usual summer walking shorts. Her white sandals had narrow, delicate straps and a one-inch heel, a compromise between dressy shoes and comfortable ones.

This morning she didn't offer to drive Clay. He'd refused her invitations enough times to make her realize that he preferred to get about on his own, even if walking was still uncomfortable. Fortunately Grace Chapel was only a short distance from the inn.

"Tell me about your minister," Clay said as they started walking to church. "How did he come to the Lord's service?"

"As I understand it," Alice said, "he came from an affluent but only nominally Christian family. In college he read Joseph Campbell and began to see the importance of a spiritual life. He attended seminary and became a minister in Boston, his hometown. Unfortunately, his wife died tragically young about ten years ago. We're greatly blessed to have him with us now. His outreach to the poor and bereaved is an example to all of us."

"I'm glad I'll get to meet him," Clay said, taking long strides in spite of his limp, which made Alice hurry to keep up.

He started to tell Alice about a minister who served his home church when he was young.

"Even after he retired, he visited nursing homes and hospitals every day. He was by my grandmother's side when she passed on. At the funeral he talked about how beautiful her face had been when she gave herself over to the Lord. I pray that she'll approve of what I'm doing with the inheritance she left me. She loved nature and tried to share it with everyone who came into her orbit."

They'd reached the chapel, and again Clay had given her something to ponder. He was such an extraordinary young man that they would all miss him when he resumed his walk.

Florence had appointed herself Clay's shepherd, greeting him outside the door and taking him to meet as many people as possible before the organ started playing to signal the beginning of the service. Ethel trailed the two of them, ignored by Florence, but Clay made a special point of including her in every conversation, however brief. He took her arm and escorted her to a separate pew after Ronald Simpson steered his wife to their accustomed place.

Alice joined Jane near the front and spent a minute in silent prayer before Rev. Thompson began the service. Her heart overflowed with gratitude for the blessings in her life, but she especially asked the Lord to watch over Clay when he resumed his long journey. She also asked for the grace and love to treat the Snypers kindly, even though part of her was still angry at their deceit.

Her mind wandered as the congregation sang and prayed, but she was startled into full concentration when she heard the theme of Rev. Thompson's sermon.

"Love your enemies and pray for those who persecute you" (Matthew 5:44), he began.

"If you love those who love you, what reward will you get? Are not even the tax collectors doing that? And if you greet only your brothers, what are you doing more than others? Do not even pagans do that?" (Matthew 5:46–47).

Alice couldn't help marveling at how often Rev. Thompson addressed her own urgent concerns in his sermons. Of all the lessons the Lord had taught His followers, the minister had chosen one that was proving particularly difficult for her at the moment.

Part of her harbored a kernel of outrage that guests under their roof had taken advantage of their hospitality. The Snypers had a right to start any kind of business they wished, but Alice still felt hurt that they had not been forthcoming about their reason for staying at the inn.

Rev. Thompson never shouted or made extravagant claims when he preached. His mellow tone matched his patrician appearance and formal, almost austere demeanor, and, most importantly, his message was always one of love. If he admonished the congregation, they accepted his admonition in the caring spirit in which it was delivered. He challenged people to look within their own souls and follow the path of righteousness for the sake of the Lord.

Alice felt a bit ashamed of the hostility she'd felt toward the Snypers even though she'd never displayed it openly. Loving an enemy meant showing genuine concern for their welfare.

When the sermon ended, she couldn't stop thinking about it. Her mind was still preoccupied with the difficulty of loving those who transgressed against her, but the Lord's message was never one of hopelessness. The spiritual rewards of following His way were great indeed. She prayed that her faith was strong enough to truly forgive anyone who did her harm.

"You were far away," Jane said when Alice was one of the last to stand up and leave after the service.

"Yes, but I'm back now," she said with a broad smile. Later she would tell Jane what so engrossed her—but maybe Jane had had a similar reaction to the words of the Gospel.

Louise was impressed by the preparations for the brunch. With Ethel's help, Florence had arranged a network to contact almost every member of the congregation, missing only those who were away on vacation. A long table in the Assembly Room was practically groaning under the weight of dishes filled with egg recipes, salads, casseroles, bacon and sausages, vegetables, fruit salads and desserts. Florence had contributed a huge platter of fried chicken. Ethel had ordered loaves of bread from the bakery and sliced them herself.

People stayed to enjoy a hearty meal, but they soon redirected their attention from delicious food to their guest of honor.

"For those who haven't met him, I'd like to introduce Perry Clay Garfield," Rev. Thompson said after saying grace. "He prefers to be called Clay by his friends, and he'll tell you about an interesting trek he's making from Nebraska to New York. First, though, let us give thanks for our wonderful brunch, made possible through the efforts of Ethel Buckley and Florence Simpson."

Louise was pleased that he'd given Ethel credit. Her aunt was beaming from the attention, and no doubt she was telling her friends all about the inn's celebrity visitor.

When most people had finished eating and some children started running and playing outside, Clay stood up and thanked first the Lord, then all the ladies who'd made the feast possible.

"Now," he said, "I'd be obliged if everyone would stand up and follow me."

After some surprised comments and much scraping of chairs, everyone, remaining children included, followed him around and around the room as though he were the Pied Piper of Hamelin.

"Everyone can sit down now," he said.

Such was his persuasive power that even toddlers obeyed by sitting on the floor where they'd stopped.

"There's nothing better for you after a big meal—or any other time—than a brisk walk," he said. "But I think everyone will agree that walking inside four walls isn't very exciting. There's a better way."

He went on to explain his mission to urge communities to lay out hiking and biking trails.

"We can't really appreciate God's gifts in nature without going outside to enjoy them. How many of you have walked through a forest or followed the path of a lazy winding river this summer? Have you climbed a mountain or even a steep hill? Do you know what treasures the Lord has provided for you right around your own town?"

He talked about nature trails, mesmerizing his audience with stories about the wonders such trails could provide. He used examples from his long walk from Nebraska, then talked about the importance of walking trails in every community.

"Sounds pretty expensive to me," Ronald Simpson said, sounding curious but not critical. "How are these trails financed?"

"In a variety of ways. It only happens when enough people want it to," Clay said before he went on to explain some of the options.

Even though Louise had already heard much of what he was saying, she was fascinated by his gift for reaching people. On the one hand, she and her sisters were upset by the Snypers, but on the other, they felt blessed to have such a charismatic young man staying with them.

Long after the tables were cleared and the food dishes covered to be taken home, a small group clustered around Clay, asking questions. Louise and Alice finally opted to go home, but Jane stayed behind, deep in conversation with Rev. Thompson, Clay and a few others.

"He's an extraordinary young man," Alice said.

"Yes, and people seem to be taking his mission to heart. I doubt that Acorn Hill has the resources to build the kind of trail he's talking about," Louise said thoughtfully, "but we're already fortunate in having quiet streets, lanes and roadways for walking. If he's convinced people to get outside and see more of God's creation, he's done a marvelous job here."

"Not to mention a boost for wellness. He's inspired Ethel and Florence to start a walking club," Alice reminded her.

"Yes, and they've recruited me to be their first new member. I wonder how that is going to work out."

Jane was sorry the brunch event was over. She had felt privileged to be part of the conversation between Rev. Thompson and Clay. Although she thought that she knew their minister quite well, she'd seen a new side of him today. Clay had tapped into the minister's deeply spiritual side, bringing out a personal testimonial of his faith.

What was it about this young man that touched people so deeply? In his presence, Ethel was less flighty and Florence was practically humble. Jane's many activities seemed less important than nurturing her soul. In fact, she hadn't once thought about her dinner plans since she'd left for church that morning.

Clay walked back to the inn with her, his step brisk in spite of his tendency to limp.

"What a blessing to have Rev. Thompson as your minister," he said.

"Yes, we're grateful to have him here. I'm sorry he can't join us this evening. I asked, but he has other plans."

"He's a lonely man," Clay said compassionately.

"He must still miss his wife," Jane said, although she didn't feel comfortable talking about her pastor and friend on such a personal level.

"The closer he embraces the Lord, the easier it becomes for him."

Jane was astonished that she was having this conversation with a young man half her age, and even more surprised that everything he said made such sense. She didn't answer because she didn't know quite what to say.

They parted company when they reached the inn, and Jane hurried to the kitchen, her mind now full of things that needed to be done before the cookout.

Louise had gone up to her room for a brief rest, but Alice waited for Jane in the kitchen. The cookout had been her idea, and Jane knew her sister wouldn't feel right unless she shared in the preparations.

"I thought you'd never get here," Alice said. "Did I miss anything by not staying longer?"

"Clay and Rev. Thompson had an interesting conversation. Those of us who stayed mostly just listened. They talked about reverence for life, among other things. Clay's home church does a blessing of the animals every spring."

"Do they actually take them inside the church?"

"Not since people started bringing sheep and horses and cows," Jane said with a smile. "It started with household pets but grew into quite a big event. Now it's held outside in a grove of trees. Clay made it sound like a lovely service."

"I know he's eager to be on his way, but we're blessed by having him here. I'm really looking forward to this evening. Thank you for taking it on. Now, dear sister, what can I do for you?"

"I boiled potatoes for the salad, but they need to be peeled and cut up."

"That's something I can handle," Alice said, not needing to point out her limited culinary skills.

"You can chop onions and celery too, and slice the eggs. I'll make the dressing. But there's no hurry. You can change clothes first."

"I'll just wear one of your big aprons."

Jane left her to the task of slicing and dicing and went upstairs to change into something more suitable for kitchen work.

Alice had hardly begun when Vera arrived. She'd insisted on bringing dessert, which she was dropping off early.

"I made graham cracker cream pie and fresh peach pie," she said, unloading her carrier and putting them in the fridge. "I wasn't sure one would be enough."

"The trouble with your pies," Alice teased, "is that everyone will want to try both, myself included."

"Just so long as you don't send any home with me. I'm my own biggest fan when it comes to pies. Can I help you with anything?"

"No, thanks. I'm just getting things ready for potato salad. It's well within my range of ability."

"You hate chopping onions," Vera said. "I never get all weepy doing them, so I'll take over for you there."

Alice was more grateful for her friend's company than for help with the onions, although she was prone to watery eyes.

"Fred remembered talking to your guest at the hardware store," Vera said. "He was very impressed with him. Not many young people take on such a big challenge for a cause. How are his feet doing?"

"One is healing well, but he had a rather severe infection in the other. I wanted to take him back to Dr. Garcia, but Clay insists on putting his faith in the Lord's healing powers. As a Christian I admire him for that, but as a nurse I can't help wanting him to get more medical care."

"Surely medicine and faith aren't at odds with each other," Vera said. "Some of our great missionaries have been doctors and nurses."

"Can I help?" Clay asked, coming to the kitchen door. "I'm a whiz at peeling potatoes."

"You needn't—" Alice started to say. Guests were not encouraged to spend time in the kitchen, but he took over the bowl of boiled potatoes before she could finish her protest.

She started slicing the celery, but before she could finish a single stalk, Isabel Snyper tapped at the entrance to the kitchen.

"I wonder—oh, I didn't know you had company," Isabel said. "I only wondered if you had a spare extension cord. My husband likes to read in bed, and I thought I could move a lamp closer."

"I'm not sure. I'll ask Jane."

"Don't go to any trouble. What are you making? Oh, I see it's potato salad. Can I help? I love cutting things up. I'm a fanatic about knives. I like mine to be razor sharp. Here, let me cut up the celery for you."

Alice started to turn her down, but there was no good reason for doing so. She remembered her resolve to love her enemies. Excluding Isabel from the group in the kitchen wouldn't be the act of a caring person. She handed over her knife.

"This is my friend Vera Humbert," she said.

The two women exchanged greetings.

"You've met Clay, of course."

"How are you, Mrs. Snyper?" he asked politely.

"Oh, just fine, Clay." Her face became more animated than Alice had ever seen it. "How do you want your celery—small, medium or large pieces?"

It wasn't something Alice had considered. "However you think they should be."

Alice intended to prepare the eggs to garnish the salad. Jane always laid them on top and sprinkled on a bit of paprika to make the salad more colorful.

"Ready to go?" Vern Snyper asked, calling out to his wife from the door.

"Oh, just give me a few minutes," Isabel said. "I'm helping with the potato salad."

"What can I do?" he asked.

"Nothing really," Alice said, trying not to sound agitated. "I think all the jobs are taken."

"I'm a genius at egg slicing," he said, moving to a spot near the counter where Alice was working.

He washed his hands at the kitchen sink and took over the slicing.

Alice stepped back and surveyed all the activity, totally without a job herself now.

"Just call me Tom Sawyer," she said with a little laugh.

"I worked my way through college helping in the dorm kitchen," Vern said, obviously enjoying his slicing.

"Shall I slice all the celery?" Isabel asked.

"Yes, I guess so." Alice felt that the whole process was out of her hands.

Clay worked quickly, filling the huge metal bowl that Jane would use to mix in the dressing after she made it. There seemed to be enough potatoes to feed a regiment.

"There, I hope these are right," Isabel said, showing them to Alice before dumping them in the bowl on top of the potatoes.

"I don't think there's any right or wrong," Vera assured her, looking a bit watery-eyed from her own efforts.

Alice didn't know quite why she was about to extend the invitation, since she still felt a bit hostile toward the Snypers, but she felt compelled.

"Maybe you two would like to join us for a cookout this evening," she suggested.

"We were going to Potterston to have dinner in a restaurant there," Isabel said, sounding a bit sorry that they had plans.

"We can do that another night," her husband said. "We'd love to come."

"Seven o'clock you said, didn't you?" Clay asked, saving Alice the necessity of telling them.

Soon all her helpers scattered, and Alice sat staring at their handiwork. What was she going to tell her sisters?

She'd just included the two people that they'd so recently considered evicting.

❧

"You did what?" Louise asked later that day.

"It seemed like the thing to do," Alice said in a hushed voice, not wanting their conversation to carry to their guests. "They helped with the potato salad."

"You did the right thing," Jane said thoughtfully. "It's not enough to give lip service to loving one's enemies."

"Will we have enough food?" Alice asked in a worried tone.

"No problem. I have lots of barbecued chicken. There should be plenty. And I'll make up a batch of the crab dip that you like so much."

Alice was reassured about the amount of food, and pleased by the promise of Jane's delicious dip, but she still felt uneasy about inviting the Snypers. It was going to test their hospitality to the utmost.

She helped set up folding tables outside and did a few things Jane needed her to do, but she still felt a bit guilty about putting so much onto her sister. Fortunately, Jane seemed to be enjoying herself, as she always did when preparing to entertain.

When it was nearly time for guests to arrive, Alice hurried upstairs and changed into white slacks and a yellow-flowered tunic, hoping to feel festive in spite of her additions to the guest list. She was just coming down the stairs when someone knocked softly on the front door.

"I'm afraid I'm early," Jody said when Alice opened the door. "It's a bad habit of mine."

"Not at all," Alice assured her. "I wish everyone was so prompt."

She'd never seen her young friend looking quite so perky. Jody was wearing a pretty feminine print skirt with rosy pink flowers that cascaded down the filmy material and swirled at midcalf. She'd wisely chosen to wear a very simple pink cotton shell and flat white pumps that showed off her slender ankles. Her curly blonde hair was hanging down to her shoulders, not restrained with clips as it was at work.

"You're looking lovely this evening," Alice added.

"I hope I'm not overdressed. I don't have much chance to dress up."

"You're perfect!"

"Thank you for saying so," the young nurse said. "I've heard about your bed-and-breakfast. This is really a lovely house."

"Let me show you around."

"I'd love that—but where should I put this?" She held out a cheese ball on a plate covered with plastic wrap. "You said it was a cookout. I thought this might go well."

"I'm sure it will. It was nice of you to bring it. Let's put it in the kitchen. Then we can see the rest of the house."

"How lovely," Jane said when Alice introduced her and Jody presented the cheese ball.

"I hope you like a touch of blue cheese. I used just one ounce to eight ounces of cream cheese and a pound of sharp cheddar, but it tends to give it an unusual flavor."

"If it tastes as good as it looks, I'll probably ask you for the recipe," Jane said with a broad smile.

"I'm going to give Jody a tour of the house before the other guests arrive," Alice explained.

She showed her the library, dining room and living room, but it was the parlor that really caught her young guest's attention.

"It's absolutely beautiful, like stepping back in time."

Jody's enthusiasm made Alice see it with fresh eyes. The wallpaper with green ivy and pale lavender violets was a wonderful background for the Victorian furnishings and the curio cabinets. The visitor was obviously charmed by the display of antique porcelain dolls and vases, but it was the baby grand piano that especially excited her attention.

"I've never known anyone who has one in her home. We have an old upright, but it's been a long time since I took lessons."

"My sister Louise gives lessons here. Sometimes she can be persuaded to play when we have guests."

When Jody was through marveling at the ambiance of the parlor, Alice invited her to take a look at the upper floors too."

She led Jody to the second floor to give her a brief look at their guest rooms.

"Only two rooms are occupied this evening," she said, "so I can show you the other two."

"I've never stayed in a bed-and-breakfast," Jody said, "but yours makes me want to vacation here. I always did love older houses, especially Victorian. This reminds me of my grandmother's, but hers is much smaller."

They stepped back into the hallway, and Alice nearly collided with Clay, who had just left his room.

"Clay Garfield, this is Jody Monroe, one of our dinner guests. Clay is staying with us a few days. He's walking from Nebraska to New York."

"It's nice to meet you, Clay."

For the first time since Alice had met him, he said absolutely nothing.

"That's an awfully long way to walk," Jody said, shrinking back behind Alice.

"Jody works with me at the hospital." Alice tried again to get some response from him. She was dumbfounded by his speechlessness.

"Nice to meet you," he finally mumbled.

Could it be that the outgoing young man was shy with girls? Alice started to feel that she'd made a big mistake. It would do nothing for Jody's self-confidence if the only guest her age at the cookout ignored her.

"Let's see if the rest of the guests are here," Alice said, virtually shooing the two of them down the stairs in front of her.

Fortunately, Vera, Fred and the Snypers had already gathered around the grill outside, enjoying glasses of iced tea and a variety of appetizers that included Jane's crab dip, a fresh vegetable platter, clam spread and crackers to go with Jody's cheese ball. Jane was in her element, waiting for the charcoal to reach the perfect temperature. Louise was chatting with Vera and Ethel, and Fred was keeping the Snypers entertained with stories about his model train hobby.

"Vern loves building historical dioramas," his wife said.

"Unfortunately I don't have much time," he said. "I'm hoping to complete a Native-American village I started years ago."

Alice introduced the two young people, and Clay went over to Fred with only a nod to the others. It wasn't the first dinner party she'd attended where men talked to men and women talked to women, but Clay had seemed so gregarious in every other situation.

She guided the young nurse around the group, trying hard to include her in the conversation. Ethel was her usual chatty self and soon learned all she could about Jody. Out of the corner of her eye, Alice saw that Clay hadn't joined in any of the conversations, instead he sat backward on a folding chair beside Fred with his eyes on the ground.

Alice made a point of talking with both Isabel and Vern, and to her relief, it wasn't as difficult as she'd anticipated. They didn't ask any more questions about Grace Chapel Inn, and she made it a point not to say a word about their plans. Even Ethel remained mute on the subject, and Fred's kindly, outgoing manner kept everyone entertained.

Jane's new barbecue recipe using molasses and green peppers along with other ingredients was a huge success. Her potato salad disappeared in no time as almost everyone had seconds—everyone except Jody and Clay. Alice worried that they weren't having a good time. Somehow they'd ended up sitting side by side, but they were eating in silence, Jody picking at her chicken and Clay pushing his portion of salad around his plate.

Having Isabel and Vern as guests didn't prove to be quite the ordeal she'd dreaded. In fact, everyone but the two young people seemed to be having a good time.

Alice lost track of them after Vera served her two wonderful pies. Dusk caught up with them, but everyone lingered in the lawn chairs, enjoying quiet conversation and the last of a spectacular sunset.

It was so unlike Jody to be impolite, but she must have felt ill at ease because she slipped away without a word of thanks to her hostesses. As for Clay, Alice had been lulled into thinking that she was getting to know him. His disappearance was even more surprising.

Everyone said their good-byes. The Humberts escorted Ethel to the carriage house, concerned that she would be walking in the dark. Vern and Isabel sounded sincerely grateful for the invitation, and Alice joined her sisters in cleaning up.

"It went well, I thought," Louise said in the kitchen. "I tried hard to treat the Snypers as I would any of our friends."

"You did splendidly," Jane assured her.

"I feel bad about Jody and Clay, though," Alice said. "They didn't seem to have any fun at all."

Jane laughed so loudly that it startled her. Louise was grinning from ear to ear.

"You don't know, do you?" Louise said.

"What?"

"They're still on the front porch deep in conversation."

Chapter Nine

*L*ouise was pleased when Ethel came into the kitchen at exactly 9:00 AM, Monday. Her aunt wasn't by nature a morning person in spite of her years as a farm wife when she had to get up to fix her family's breakfast. It boded well for their walking club that she had made the effort to be on time.

"Aunt Ethel, may I get you some breakfast?" Jane asked.

"Oh no, thank you, dear. You probably have guests to feed. I don't want to take up your time."

"I don't expect anyone down for breakfast for another hour, so it's no trouble at all."

Louise had opted to have juice and a piece of toast before setting off, but Ethel was adamant about not wanting anything before she walked.

"I have my water bottle," she said, pulling it from the deep side pocket of her white overalls.

She was wearing them over a silky long-sleeved blouse, an extremely unusual combination. The overalls were so crisp and clean that Louise suspected her aunt had bought them just for walking. Her white-and-black striped athletic shoes looked brand new too, as did a jaunty little cap with a visor, and sunglasses in a mock tortoise-shell frame.

"Florence and I worked out the route we should follow," Ethel said. "She had Ronald drive the distance in his car to get the exact mileage. We thought two miles would be a nice beginning. Then we'll work up to longer distances."

"Are you sure you want to go that far the first day?" Jane asked with concern. "It will start to get hot before you get home."

"That's why we're heading out early, to take advantage of the morning coolness," Ethel said. "I do hope Florence gets here soon. I know she's as eager to start as I am, and she's usually so prompt."

Just then the sound of a car door slamming summoned them all to the back door. Florence had parked her car in the inn's lot and was eager to begin her trek.

"Are you girls ready to go?" she called, standing next to her car.

Florence, too, had procured a new outfit for walking. She was wearing bright pink cotton slacks and a roomy pink and white striped crinkled-cotton shirt that hung nearly to her knees. She'd thought to bring a hat too, a wide-brimmed straw one with a big white bow. Her walking shoes, like Ethel's, were too dazzlingly white to be anything but new. The effect of her casual outfit was somewhat spoiled by a dark brown belt around her waist that held a holster for her water bottle and a fanny pack. Her sun goggles reminded Louise of those worn by early aviators, but they would certainly do the job of shielding her eyes.

Louise felt a bit drab in her old khaki skirt and a white boatneck top. Her shoes were well-scuffed but reliably comfortable, and she hoped the other two wouldn't regret walking in footwear that hadn't been broken in.

"I thought we could drive to the firehouse and park on the side street, where the car won't be in the way," Florence said. "Then we'll walk down Berry Lane to Village Road and continue on. I had Ronald put out a plastic marker, one of those garden sticks, at the one-mile mark. That's where we'll turn around."

The logic of driving to begin a walk made Louise smile to herself, but obviously the other two women had put a lot of thought into this first outing. She didn't want to say anything that would dampen their enthusiasm, although she did wonder whether her aunt was up for two miles the first time.

"Tallyho!" Florence called, gesturing for them to get into the car.

Her plan hit its first setback when the parking spot she'd intended to use was occupied. She circled around the block three times hoping it would be free, but Louise finally persuaded Florence to take one a bit farther down the street.

"We can stop that much short of your marker," Louise assured her. "I'm good at judging distances."

She really hadn't had much need to judge distances, but they were wasting the cool part of the morning looking for the perfect parking place.

Louise helped her aunt out of the car and started walking side by side with her while Florence marched ahead a few steps, explaining how she'd had to get shoes a size larger than usual to accommodate her bunion. She'd only gone a block or so when her monologue started sounding a bit breathless.

The three walked in silence until they came to the intersection of Berry Lane and Acorn Avenue. Ahead of them, Betty, the manager and head beautician of Clip 'n' Curl, was outside polishing the glass door of her shop.

"My, you ladies are out early this morning," she called to them.

"We've formed a walking club," Florence was quick to explain. "It looks like you're an early riser too. Maybe you would like to join us."

"It sounds like fun," Betty said, "but this is the only time of day I'm free to catch up on jobs around the shop."

Louise kept walking after a quick good morning to the beautician, then paused when she realized that both

Florence and Ethel had stayed to talk to her. Florence wanted to know if she could change her next appointment time, and Betty assured her that she could if she phoned any time that day. Ethel wanted her to check out her hair color in the sunlight to see if it should be darkened just a little.

Expecting the other two to follow, Louise crossed to the front of the Presbyterian church on Village Road, then looked back. Her walking companions were still chatting with Betty. Was the conversation really important, or were both of them already in need of a short rest? Louise tried to wait patiently, but she did want to get on with the walk.

The morning was still pleasantly cool with just enough breeze to ruffle Louise's short silver hair as she walked. When the other two eventually caught up, Louise led them down the road toward the Dairyland gas station and convenience store.

"You know, I'm really sorry I didn't bring a can of that lemon drink I like so much," Ethel said. "It quenches my thirst so much better than plain water."

"Well, here's your chance to get one," Florence said. "As a matter of fact, I'm beginning to regret skipping breakfast. Maybe I'll run in and buy one of those packets of miniature doughnuts. They're hardly a bite each, so I don't see what harm it would do to have an energy boost."

Louise declined to go into the store with them, but again they lingered. She could see them through the front door, talking to the young clerk as though she were a long-lost relative. Louise glanced at her watch, wondering how long it should take to walk two miles. At the rate they were going, it would take all morning.

At last her two companions came out of the store and began walking resolutely down the road, Ethel sipping her drink and Florence nibbling on doughnuts covered with powdered sugar. Since her two companions had declined her offer to share them, she polished off the packet herself. To her credit, Florence stuffed the wrapper in her fanny pack instead of throwing it on the ground. This required another stop while she unzipped and rezipped it, then lectured a bit about the virtues of not littering.

Louise sighed, hoping this was the last delay. She had lessons to plan for the week and errands to run. It hadn't occurred to her that a morning walk would take quite so long.

Since their route was taking them along the shoulder of the road, they walked single file with Florence in the lead and Ethel bringing up the rear. Louise kept looking back to see whether her aunt was keeping up. They'd hardly gone a hundred yards when Ethel started to fall behind. Louise slowed her own pace and called ahead to Florence to wait a bit.

"Are you all right?" Louise asked.

"Yes, of course. You forget my legs are shorter than yours."

Louise had forgotten her experiences shopping with her aunt. The kindest way to describe Ethel's usual pace was "deliberate." She was one of those people who just didn't believe in moving quickly.

"We can turn back if this route is a little long for the first time," Louise offered.

"Goodness no! We've planned how far we'll walk very carefully. Florence has lots of magazines telling how to keep in shape. I certainly won't be the one to quit before we reach our goal."

"Walking is great exercise," Louise said, "but it's always a good idea to start slowly. A mile is a perfectly respectable distance for a beginner."

"I don't really think of myself as a beginner," her aunt said, sounding a bit miffed. "I walk to the shops all the time."

Florence had walked back to see what the delay was.

"Why can't I be the leader for a while?" Ethel asked.

Her friend wasn't enthusiastic about that idea, but she reluctantly allowed Ethel to take her place at the head of the trio.

"Do set a lively pace, Ethel. You know a walk has to be brisk to do any good," Florence said.

"This is only our first morning. You can't expect me to sprint."

Florence took the number-two position and Louise brought up the rear, slowly strolling behind the others so she didn't pass them.

"Oh, drat!" Florence gave a little hop that would've been funny if she hadn't immediately plopped down in obvious distress on a grassy patch beside the road.

"Are you hurt?" Ethel asked with alarm.

"No, just a stone in my shoe, I think," she said, unlacing it.

She shook her new walking shoe and explored the inside without finding anything.

"Once I bought a pair of shoes that had a nail sticking up through the sole," Ethel said. "You can bet I returned them to the store in a hurry."

"I can't find anything. Maybe it was just a stabbing pain from my bunion," Florence said, sticking her foot out to show them the impressive bulge beside her big toe.

"Maybe we'd better call it a day," Louise said. "I could go back to the convenience store and call Jane to come for us."

"No, no, no," Florence said vehemently. "We set a goal, and I won't be the one to let everyone down."

Since "everyone" was just Louise and her aunt, Louise doubted "anyone" would be disappointed to return home now. But she had agreed to join their club. In fact, she felt responsible for getting them home safely.

"Give me a hand, would you please?" Florence asked the two of them. "It's hard to get up with nothing to hang on to."

Louise took one hand and Ethel the other, both of them pulling with all their strength until Florence was upright again.

"You see why it's so important to walk in a group," she said after thanking them. "If I were here alone, I would be in a pickle."

Louise was eager to get to the mile-marker. The day was getting warmer, and Ethel was looking flushed. She wished that she'd checked to be sure her aunt had put on protective sunscreen, but, of course, both of them expected to be through with the walk by the time the sun was high in the sky.

"We should see Ronald's marker soon," Florence said after a few more minutes of walking. "I want to be sure to take it back with us. Otherwise it would be littering."

"What color is it?" Ethel asked slightly breathlessly as they went up a small incline in the road. "My, I need to stop for a drink."

"It's just a white stick, actually, but I thought it would show up well."

"Maybe we passed it without noticing," Ethel said hopefully.

"No, I'm sure I would have seen it," Florence insisted.

"Why don't the two of you take a little break, and I'll see if I can spot it ahead," Louise suggested.

"No, I'd better go. You don't know what it looks like," Florence reasoned. "It can't possibly be far now. We've been walking forever."

Louise had to agree that it felt like an exceedingly long trek, thanks to all the delays and time-outs, but she doubted that they had covered a mile yet.

"Tallyho!" Florence called out—this time with several decibels less enthusiasm—then took the lead again with no protest from Ethel.

Louise wasn't sure why a fox-hunting term had become Florence's marching call, but at the moment she was mainly concerned with getting her aunt back to a shady place before the sun got any hotter. Whether Florence liked it or not, she was calling Jane for a ride as soon as they got back to the convenience store where she could use a phone. Ethel had delicate skin, and she was older than Louise or Florence. It didn't make sense for her to overdo her exercise.

They slowly made their way along the road, passed occasionally by a car. Someone Florence knew stopped and offered a lift, but she waved her on.

"Thanks, but this is our walking club," she said.

Louise gave Florence high marks for fortitude, but she was beginning to worry that something had happened to the marker. Maybe a conscientious citizen had stopped and taken it, assuming that it was debris.

"There it is! There it is!" Florence cried out in excitement. "We're halfway to our goal." She hurried down another slope in the road, this one the steepest yet.

Louise was concerned that Ethel might be in danger of passing out. She was dragging behind again, looking much too red in the face. As far as she knew, her aunt was in good health for her age—which she never revealed although she had to be in her seventies.

"You can retrieve it," Louise said to Florence. "We'll wait for you here."

"I want to go the full distance," Ethel protested rather weakly.

"You've had a great walk for the first day. I'm going to call Jane as soon as we get back to the convenience store. She'll give us a ride home."

"Oh dear, Florence won't like that."

Louise wasn't so sure of that. Their friend had the marker and was waving it like a trophy, but she was moving very slowly, limping a little as she made her way up the steep dip in the road.

"Got it!" Florence said, huffing and puffing from the climb. "Maybe next time we can pick a flatter route. It didn't seem so hilly riding in the car."

"We've had a good idea," Louise said, tactfully including Ethel. "Since it's promising to be an unusually warm day, we can call Jane from the convenience store to come get us."

"But our goal for today was two miles," Florence persisted—though not very strenuously.

"One mile plus is a very good start. It wouldn't hurt to build up gradually, especially since we're having such a hot spell. Your face is almost as red as Ethel's."

"You're probably right." Florence tried to sound grudging, but Louise could detect relief in her voice. "Maybe next time we should walk in town. Then if we feel flushed, there are places to stop."

"Good idea." Louise took her aunt's arm and started back. She could hear Florence breathing hard behind them.

The convenience store still seemed far away, especially since they were walking at a turtle's pace, but at last they went into the cool interior, where they could use a phone.

"Dear, I don't have any money with me," Louise said.

"Oh, I always carry mad money," Florence said, digging a coin purse out of her fanny pack. "One never knows what will come up."

"If you don't have the right change, I'll ask the clerk to break my five dollar bill," Ethel said.

The rascals, Louise thought. *They'd both come prepared to bail if necessary.*

She smiled as she went to call Jane.

Jane wasn't in the least surprised to get Louise's call for a ride. In fact, she'd started to wonder where the walkers were, suspecting that maybe they'd stopped for breakfast before coming home.

Clay was in the kitchen with her. He'd been there since breakfast, volunteering to help her and telling her more about his unusual walking project as he worked. Jane was fascinated by his experiences, so much so that she let some of her chores wait while she listened to him.

He loaded the dishwasher, swept the floor and took out the trash, doing it all in such a natural way that it didn't seem inappropriate to let a guest help so much.

"I'm going to pick up my sister and aunt," Jane said after Louise's call.

"What else can I do for you?" Clay asked. "I have plenty of time on my hands."

He seemed so eager to help that Jane didn't want to turn down his offer.

"Do you have a valid driver's license?"

"A Nebraska license, yes."

"Would you mind taking my car to pick up my sister and aunt at the convenience store on Village Road? Mrs. Simpson is with them too. She'll need a ride to her car near the fire department. It would be a big help to me."

"I'll be glad to," he said, his face animated by the prospect of being helpful.

Jane gave him the key to her car, and directions on how to find the walkers.

"Oh, I have an idea," she added. "I don't have anywhere to go today. Why don't you borrow my car later, maybe go over to Potterston? I'm afraid you won't find very much to keep you occupied in Acorn Hill."

"You wouldn't mind?" he asked excitedly. "The doctor did recommend that I buy some hiking boots."

"Not at all. In fact, keep it as long as you like after you bring my family home. Maybe you'd like to have dinner in Potterston and see a movie or something."

"Terrific! I can't tell you how much I appreciate it. I'll take good care of your car."

"I don't doubt it."

Louise's call had been a blessing in disguise. Jane was fascinated by the stories of Clay's walk across the Midwest, but it wouldn't be right to let him work for her all day when he was a guest. He did strike her as a person who enjoyed being with people and keeping active. She was delighted that she'd thought of offering him the use of her car, especially since she had to give all her attention to the plans for tomorrow's breakfast. They were scheduled to have a full house that night.

"I'll fill it up with gas too," he called back as he was leaving. "Thanks so much!"

Jane got to work in earnest and had just put two loaves of oatmeal bread in pans to rise when Louise came into the kitchen looking a bit frazzled.

"Did Aunt Ethel go home?" Jane asked.

"Yes, the poor dear. She badly needs to cool down. Both she and Florence were a little too optimistic about their first walk."

"Are they okay?"

"Yes, it just got warmer than either of them expected. Of course, we moved too slowly. It was hot before we'd only gone half the distance they wanted to go."

"I never thought of our aunt as a fast mover."

"It wasn't just that we walked too slowly. They stopped to talk, to eat, to drink. Florence had foot trouble, and the heat was getting to Aunt Ethel."

"It doesn't sound like you had much fun."

"I spent most of the time waiting for them. Jane, how am I going to get out of their club without hurting their feelings?"

"At least you were along to look after Aunt Ethel. Whose idea was it to call me?"

"Mine. They planned to walk two miles today. Florence made Ronald put out a stake as their mile-marker."

"You're going to have to keep an eye on them, aren't you?" Jane asked in a practical voice. "What if you hadn't been with them? Do you think they would have tried to finish the whole two miles?"

She knew the answer to that. Once Florence set a goal, she was usually unstoppable, and she'd certainly managed to convince Ethel to join her. Louise had to be a member of the walking club until they disbanded. She didn't want them stranded along the road, unable to go on.

"Maybe Alice can give them some wellness tips and help them set reasonable goals," Louise said.

"Good luck on that!" Jane countered, scooping up the cat as he sidled up to her ankles.

Alice checked her watch again and frowned. If there was one thing she'd learned in her years of nursing, it was not to keep a doctor waiting. Still, she hated to go to his office without Jody. The young nurse had the tape recorder, and it would be her responsibility to write the article. Alice hoped that she wouldn't have to do the interview without her, but Dr. Jackson was so busy that she would be embarrassed to cancel their appointment. He was the hospital's leading specialist in cardiovascular diseases, and she felt privileged to be able to include him in the first wellness newsletter.

Could Jody possibly have forgotten? It didn't seem likely. Perhaps she'd been called upon to help with an emergency. Certainly that was an everyday occurrence in their line of work. Still, it was odd that Jody hadn't sent word with another employee if she couldn't keep her appointment.

They were already a few minutes late, and Alice made up her mind to meet with the doctor by herself. She was about to knock on the closed door of his office when Jody came running toward her.

"I'm so sorry. Something came up just as I was signing out."

She had a cell phone in one hand and the recorder in the other, but there was no time for explanations. Alice knocked briskly, and Dr. Jackson called out for them to come in.

Alice knew him well. He'd been at the hospital for more than twenty years, and like many of the other nurses, she stood a bit in awe of his ability. He was easily one of the most intelligent people on the staff, but he wasn't the most patient. He demanded the utmost from the nursing staff, and it wasn't unknown for him to reduce a novice nurse to tears. Still, he could be charming when he wasn't pressured by patient care, and he greeted Alice cordially, reminding her a little of Jimmy Stewart in one of his movies.

"Alice, so they've made you an editor."

"A very inexperienced one, I'm afraid, Dr. Jackson. Fortunately I have a writer to help me. This is Jody Monroe—"

"Of course, I had Jody on my floor for a while. She pulled a double shift when I had an especially dicey case."

Alice remembered that Dr. Jackson was one of the few physicians to call every employee by name.

"So what exactly do you require of me?" he asked, never one to spend much time being sociable.

"Unless you have a better idea, I thought we'd do a piece on heart health for women. Jody will tape our interview, if you don't mind."

"Excellent. I have a lot to say, so Jody will need to tape. I know I'm preaching to the choir, Alice, but more women over sixty-five die of cardiovascular disease than all the cancers combined. It's the number-one cause of death in that age group, number two in women ages forty-five to sixty-four, and number three in women ages twenty-five to forty-four."

"This is a staff newsletter, so we especially want to reach younger women and emphasize prevention," Alice said.

"Anyone working here should have the background to know about heart disease," he said, "but you and I know that health-care workers can be more careless than the general public when it comes to taking care of themselves. When was the last time you had a thorough physical, Alice?"

"I'm due," she said.

"Overdue, more likely, if you're anything like ninety percent of the staff here. Take care of other people and neglect themselves. Boggles the mind."

This interview wasn't going at all the way Alice had planned. But then, Dr. Jackson was always outspoken. There was a reason why he was the terror of young nurses. She noticed that Jody kept her distance and kept silent.

"You know the contributing factors," he said.

Alice was at least thankful that he was treating her as a knowledgeable professional. She asked several of her pre-planned questions, and he didn't talk down to her in his answers.

"Abdominal obesity, high blood pressure and elevated blood glucose and triglycerides are major danger signs," he said summing up. "Mental stress and depression affect women's hearts more than men's, according to some convincing studies. Smoking seems to be a lot worse for women than men. Makes me crazy to see patients outside in all weather having a cigarette in their hospital gowns because they can't smoke inside."

"Maybe the article should include the differences in symptoms between men and women," Alice suggested.

"I've got some literature you can take along," the doctor said, glancing at his wristwatch. "I want you to emphasize that women's symptoms can differ from the chest pain and pressure that men commonly experience. A woman can have pain in her neck, shoulder, upper back or abdomen. Shortness of breath, nausea or vomiting, sweating, lightheadedness, dizziness and unusual fatigue also are warning signs. Of course, knowing all this doesn't amount to a hill of beans if the patient isn't willing to make some lifestyle changes. More exercise, weight loss, healthy eating habits and regular checkups—that's what's needed. And if a doctor prescribes medication, the patient should take it. Nothing vexes me more than someone who loads up on useless preparations from a so-called health store and doesn't fill my prescriptions to lower blood pressure and cholesterol."

"I'm sure we can work all that into the article," Alice said, sensing that they were already over the time Dr. Jackson had allotted for the interview.

"Good idea, a wellness newsletter."

It was high praise coming from this doctor, and Alice quickly thanked him for his time and made ready to leave.

He had one more point to make.

"You know, Alice, for years all the research went into cardiovascular health for men. It's high time women got more attention."

"I agree, Dr. Jackson." She smiled and ushered Jody out of the office.

When they reached the parking lot, Jody let out a big sigh. "Dr. Jackson scares me."

"You and a lot of other nurses," Alice said sympathetically.

"But not you?"

"Not anymore. When he's abrupt or impatient, I just tell myself that we're on the same team. We want the same thing, our patients' recovery. Here, take the literature he gave us."

"Well, I'll see you tomorrow," Jody said, grabbing the manila envelope and abruptly hurrying away.

Alice was a bit surprised. She thought Jody might have questions about the article. In fact, she'd never seen her hurry off so fast.

A few moments later she spotted a familiar-looking blue compact pulling out of the lot. It was the first time she could remember seeing a car exactly like Jane's in the hospital parking area. There weren't that many around anymore.

Chapter Ten

I wonder how much longer Clay will stay," Jane said Tuesday morning.

Alice had the day off, so she was helping her sister with breakfast. Since she had a flexible schedule, her days off varied from week to week.

"He hasn't spoken about his blisters lately," Alice said, "and he certainly is moving a lot better. My guess is that they're nearly healed. I imagine he'll be leaving soon."

"I only ask because I have reservations for all the rooms Friday evening. Until then his room is available. Do you think I should mention it to him? "

"Let's wait a day or two. I don't want him to feel that we're trying to rush him. And who knows, maybe the Snypers will leave before then."

"Perhaps you're right."

"Oh, by the way," said Alice, "there's something I forgot to tell you. I saw a car exactly like yours in the hospital parking lot yesterday as I was leaving for home, same color, same make, same age as far as I could tell from a distance. It rather stood out among all the newer models."

Jane chuckled and looked coy.

"What?" her sister asked.

"It probably was my car. I lent it to Clay for the day. He didn't have anything to do around here. I thought it would be good therapy for him."

"Maybe he went to have his feet checked."

"I think not," Jane said, still grinning.

"What—oh dear, I wasn't expecting romance when I asked Jody to the cookout. In fact, they didn't seem to pay any attention to each other when they met, but Jody is shy. Perhaps Clay is too when it comes to young ladies, but maybe we just missed something. They did seem to be enjoying each other's company before the evening was over. Do you think Clay went to the hospital to meet her after work?"

"That's my theory."

"Now that I recall, she was in a big hurry to get away after our interview with Dr. Jackson."

"Who was in a big hurry?" Louise asked, coming into the kitchen.

"Jody," Alice said. "It appears that Clay picked her up after her shift yesterday."

"Well, it's nice that he's made a friend," Louise said pragmatically.

"I just hope she won't be too disappointed when he leaves," Alice said. "I should know better than to play matchmaker—not that it was my intention."

"Well, it's out of our hands," Jane said, taking a table knife to check the quiche baking in the oven. "Not quite done."

The first guests could be heard coming down the stairs, and Alice went into the dining room with a tray of fresh fruit cups.

"I'm sorry I can't stay to help," Louise said. "I promised to walk again. Ethel should be here any minute, and we're meeting Florence at the chapel."

"I do hope it goes better than yesterday," Jane said sympathetically.

"Good morning, ladies," Clay said, tapping on the frame of the dining room door. "Can I help with anything?"

"Good morning," Jane said cheerfully. "You might give some encouragement to Louise. She's part of a walking group, as of yesterday."

"Did you have a problem?" he asked.

"Not really, I suppose. Aunt Ethel and Florence Simpson planned the walk, and it proved to be a bit too ambitious for them."

"And more than a little pokey for Louise," Jane explained. "She walks frequently already, so the pace was awfully slow for her."

"It's good to start slowly," Clay said thoughtfully. "Why don't I join you? Maybe I can give the ladies some pointers."

"What a wonderful idea!" Ethel said, coming into the kitchen without being heard, thanks to her thick-soled walking shoes. "We'd be thrilled to have you. We've started a walking club, but so far it's just the three of us."

"Are you sure your feet are up to it?" Louise asked, wanting to give Clay an out if he regretted his impulsive offer.

"Wouldn't you like breakfast first?" Jane asked, with the same intent.

"No, thanks. I'll get something later. My feet are coming along pretty well. Just let me go upstairs and put on the new hiking boots I bought yesterday. This will be a good opportunity to test them."

"He is such a nice young man," Ethel said after he had left.

"Yes," Louise agreed. "Oh, I forgot to ask you yesterday. Did you put a good coat of sunscreen on your face and neck?"

"Of course. I know the sun could make me look wrinkled and old."

Louise knew that wasn't the main purpose of sunscreen, but she was glad her aunt was using it for whatever reason. Fair skin like hers was very susceptible to cancer. Ethel had also protected herself with a plainer version of Florence's straw hat and a long-sleeved blue striped shirt that looked like a man's dress shirt. She'd rolled the sleeves, but it still looked too big.

Alice came back to the kitchen for the bread platter, announcing that two couples were ready for breakfast.

Louise had a quick glass of apple juice, and Ethel chatted as Jane took her quiche out of the oven. Clay was back in minutes, willing to postpone his breakfast, and ready to go.

Clay offered Ethel his arm as they walked to the chapel.

"The path is a little uneven," he said to make her comfortable accepting his help.

Louise had to smile at the contrast between their heights. Her aunt looked like a little doll beside the very tall young man, his blond hair covered by the cowboy hat he used on his trek.

Florence was standing outside the chapel, slowly pacing back and forth in front of the door. They were a few minutes late, and no doubt she'd quickly grown impatient having to wait. When she saw Ethel approaching with Clay, her scowl was replaced by a wide grin.

"Clay is going to walk with our club this morning," Ethel happily announced. "We had to wait for him to put on his new hiking boots. With new boots and improved feet, he'll make a fine companion."

"Oh, it's a club," he said with a grin.

"We're just getting started," Florence assured him. "I'm certain that many others will join us once they see how much fun we're having."

Louise tried to remember any part of yesterday's walk that qualified as "fun" for Florence, deciding that maybe the powdered doughnuts counted. She had to give her credit, though, for giving it another try.

"For this morning," Florence went on, "I'm happy to say that Carlene Moss will also be joining us. She's the editor of Acorn Hill's weekly newspaper, Clay. She can only walk a little ways because tomorrow the paper comes out, and she is busy. But she said if we stop by her house, she'll join us as far as her office. It's only an itty-bitty distance, but everyone has to start somewhere."

They began walking, Ethel retaining a firm grip on Clay's arm. Not to be left out, Florence took his other one.

Louise was momentarily tempted to go home and let the three of them have their walk, but part of her was curious to see how it would go today.

Ethel and Florence had picked up the pace since yesterday. Louise was hopeful that she might yet get a good walk herself.

"My Bob never wanted to walk anywhere," Ethel was saying. "He worked so hard on the farm, of course, that he was content to sit in his rocker and read the science and mechanics magazines. He loved finding new ideas. Sometimes he'd even putter around at his workbench and make something work."

Florence, not to be outdone by her friend and some-time rival, chatted on about the things her husband liked, although she didn't mention that he loved an easy chair and a good pipe of tobacco.

From her vantage point behind them, Louise was happy to see that Clay didn't seem to be limping anymore. She would have felt bad if this little excursion caused him difficulty.

Carlene was waiting outside her house, and Florence made a big to-do about introducing her to Clay. She loos-ened her grip on his arm so he could shake hands with the editor, but Ethel clung on, not about to be displaced.

The group strolled on, moving slower than Louise might have wished, but the paved city walkway was less worrisome when it came to her aunt, not that she could possibly fall while attached to Clay's arm. Florence jockeyed for posi-tion, but Carlene maneuvered to take her place on Clay's right side.

"You're the famous walker," she said.

"Not famous, really. I'm just trying to promote interest in hiking and biking trails."

He explained his mission to Carlene, and Florence fell back to walk with Louise.

"He's such a charming young man," she whispered when the others had gotten a bit ahead. "How long is he going to stay?"

"I'm not sure. I imagine he'll continue his cross-country walk as soon as his feet are up to it."

"I've had a great idea, an article about the purpose of Clay's walk," Carlene called back. "I can't do it until late afternoon, but he's agreed to come by the office around four."

"Good plan," Louise said.

Florence was uncharacteristically quiet.

They left Carlene in front of the newspaper office, then turned to go past the police station. This morning they only walked down Village Road as far as the Methodist church, neither Ethel nor Florence showing any interest in a stop farther down the road at the convenience store.

Somewhat to Louise's surprise, they were moving at quite a respectable pace, resisting all opportunities to stop or visit with passersby. Instead of heading back to the inn, they went south on Acorn Drive and circled around the western part of town, going a greater distance than they had the morning before.

They ended up walking Florence back to Grace Chapel where her car was parked.

"That was such a lovely walk. I do hope you can join us again before you leave," Florence said.

"It would be my pleasure," he said, "but my plans are a little uncertain."

"I have an idea," she said brightly. "Why don't you come and have supper with my husband and me this evening? He's going out to a roadside market for fresh sweet corn. We'd love to have you join us. You too, Ethel and Louise," she said as a seeming afterthought.

"That's awfully kind of you, Mrs. Simpson, but I'm afraid I already have plans for this evening."

"Well, maybe another time if you're staying longer," she said, not quite able to mask her disappointment.

"Thank you for asking and for letting me join you this morning," he said with so much warmth in his voice that Florence's glum expression disappeared.

Louise watched her walk to her car, hobbling for the first time this morning. If her bunion had hurt the whole time, she'd concealed it well so that Clay wouldn't notice. What was it about this young man that made older women act like young girls around him? Ethel didn't release her grip on his arm until they were back at the inn.

What plans did he have for the evening? Was he fibbing to avoid hurting Florence's feelings? Louise didn't think so.

⌒

"How was your walk?" Alice asked as Louise, Ethel and Clay came into the kitchen.

"How could it be anything but good with such nice company?" Clay said gallantly.

"I do believe we walked farther than yesterday, only we stayed in town where it's flat and there are good walkways," Ethel said.

"What can I make for your breakfast?" Jane asked.

"Oh, don't go to any trouble for me. I'll just go home and have some toast," Ethel said.

"Aunt Ethel, when has cooking ever been a problem for me?" Jane admonished her with a big smile. "The guests pretty much demolished my first breakfast, but it won't take any time to make scrambled eggs with mushrooms. I'll grate some cheese on top if that sounds good to you."

The three walkers enthusiastically agreed, and Jane began assembling her ingredients.

"Carlene is going to interview Clay for the paper," Louise said. "She walked with us from her house to the office."

"What a good idea," Alice said. "I wonder what her hook will be."

"Hook?" Ethel asked with a puzzled frown.

"An idea to pin the story on. I'd like to be a little mouse listening to that interview," Alice said.

"Why not just come with me?" Clay asked.

"Oh, I don't know." Alice was reluctant to horn in on Carlene's interview.

"I'll call her to be sure it's okay," Clay said.

"I can't imagine that it won't be," Ethel said, sounding a bit wistful, as though she would like to go too. "I have a meeting at the chapel myself."

"I filled up your gas tank yesterday and checked the oil and water in your car, Jane. One tire was a little low, so I put air in it."

"That's awfully nice of you, Clay, but you didn't need to go to all that trouble. Still, since it's your gas in the car, maybe you'd like to borrow it again this evening."

"That would be great!" His smile was so broad that it made Jane feel especially glad that she had made her offer.

The group scattered after breakfast, and Alice went upstairs. Her own room needed some attention. Like Jane, she tended to take care of the rest of the inn before she cleaned her bedroom. Louise, of course, always kept her personal space immaculate.

It occurred to Alice that she should have gone walking with Louise and the others. The day was promising to be another scorcher, but maybe Vera would like to go out at dusk if the day cooled off a bit by then. She couldn't help smiling when she thought about her aunt's "club," but they did have a good idea. People who exercised together were probably more apt to keep it up than a solitary walker. One thing that had come out in both of her interviews for the wellness newsletter was that regular exercise was crucial. Fortunately she enjoyed her walks with Vera so much that she rarely thought of them as a chore.

The hours flew by as they always did when she had a day off, but Alice was glad that Carlene had called to invite her to the interview. Clay had asked the editor, but she'd wanted to extend a personal invitation.

"Would you prefer to ride?" she asked Clay when they met to go to the newspaper office.

"No, thank you. It feels good to stretch my legs."

Alice liked a brisk walk, but she was hard-pressed to keep up with Clay's long stride. From what she could tell, he wasn't favoring either foot. Her professional guess was that his blisters were healing nicely. Did that mean he planned to leave soon?

Carlene came out of her office to meet them and led them back to the crowded and somewhat cluttered cubicle she used as her base of operations. The temperature inside was cooler than outside, but she was obviously saving energy and money by keeping the air-conditioning set below full power.

"I think our readers will be really interested in your trek," Carlene said. "What gave you the idea?"

Clay settled back on one of the two chairs with wicker seats that she'd provided, his legs stretching halfway across the room.

"I've always been interested in history, especially the American West. The early settlers didn't ride west. They hoofed it beside their covered wagons, keeping an eye out for hostiles and game."

"But you chose to walk east."

He grinned. "There aren't many towns in Nebraska once you get west of Kearney, not ones big enough to build walking trails. I can't generate interest in building them unless there are people to hear about it."

Alice was fascinated listening to a pro elicit information. Carlene had certainly been quick to put Clay at ease, which had been the crucial first step in the advice she'd given Alice.

"Do you mind if I use my recorder?" Carlene asked Clay.

"Not at all, ma'am."

Carlene didn't have any written questions that Alice could see, but there was obviously a structure to her interview. Before long she'd learned about Clay's early interest in ecology, his parents' jobs teaching zoology and botany, and his admiration for the grandmother who had made his trip possible.

Even though Alice had heard most of Clay's story before, she acknowledged Carlene's skill in bringing out small human interest details. There certainly was an art to interviewing, and Alice realized that she'd let Dr. Jackson breeze through her interview with him without revealing any personal ties to his work. She'd never thought to ask him how he became interested in cardiovascular work, although she now saw that this was a major omission. After all, there were few things that interested people more than other people's personal stories.

Carlene's interview lasted much longer than either of Alice's, partly because the editor's questions were interesting to Clay. He was willing to tell her everything she wanted to know and even added a few details without any prompting. The longer it lasted, the more Alice felt like a rank amateur, which, of course, she was. If the first two articles in the wellness newsletter were good, it would be because Jody was a good writer, able to make a story out of fragmented interviews.

"That was a wonderful interview," she said, softly complimenting Carlene when Clay walked ahead of her to the door.

"He's a delightful subject," the editor assured her. "A nice change from school board meetings and some of the area politicians running for office."

Jane appreciated it when departing guests reported anything wrong with their rooms, but she did wish the couple had remembered sooner. As it was, she received a phone call from them in late afternoon after they'd driven for quite a few hours.

"We forgot to tell you, but we thought you might appreciate a heads-up," the wife said over the crackling noise on her cell phone. "The shower drips."

"I didn't notice when I was in the room," Jane said.

"That's the problem. It only leaks some of the time. I found myself lying awake, waiting for it to start up again.

"Well, thank you for telling me," she said checking her watch.

Jane hurried up the stairs and entered the suspect room. The guests had been right. As soon as she got near the shower, she heard the ping of water on the drain. It was indeed leaking, and the room was reserved by one of their regulars, a salesman who usually arrived around seven when his workday was over.

A dripping showerhead could be maddening, especially when a person was trying to sleep. There was no alternative. Jane had to find a plumber right away, even if it meant paying overtime.

She immediately phoned the firm that regularly serviced the inn, but all she got was an answering machine. To her dismay, it was after five, and the woman who worked in the office must have gone home.

There wasn't a choice of plumbers in Acorn Hill, so she tried several Potterston companies with the same results. She could leave a message, but there was no way to know when an actual plumber might take the call. Her only chance was to reach their regular man at home, much as she hated to bother him after hours.

To her immense agitation, all she got was a recording at his home. The family had left on a camping trip. Would she please call the number given? Unfortunately, it was one of the Potterston plumbers she'd already tried.

What would she do if there was a serious emergency like a flooded basement or a broken water pipe? She made a few more calls, this time going even farther afield, but the only plumber who actually picked up the phone refused to come after hours for a minor problem like a leaking shower.

She could hear the piano through the open door of the parlor as Louise gave a lesson, but it wouldn't do any good to consult with her sister. She knew even less than Jane did about plumbing.

Her last resort was to consult a home handyman book in her father's library. Daniel had been willing to try repairs on his own, sometimes a necessary economy in the process of raising three daughters on his ministerial salary. Jane's mother had passed away before she was old enough to know her, and sometimes money was tight keeping up a large house on a single paycheck.

Jane found the book, and it did provide some information on leaky showers. Fortunately there were illustrations that she could follow as she worked. First she had to turn off the water, then pry off the cap on the faucet handle with a small pocket knife.

She could do that!

Then she had to loosen the handle screw, remove it and pull off the stop tube.

So far, she understood the steps, but then it got tricky. There was a cartridge with a retaining clip. That had to be removed too. If she managed to pull out the cartridge with pliers, she had to buy an identical cartridge to replace the old one. If! Her father's book suggested that she might need a special cartridge puller.

Would Fred have a new cartridge in stock? Would he have a puller-thing? Was he still at the hardware store?

No time to panic, she told herself.

She called the store, but Fred didn't answer. At worst, she might have to drive to the big home supply store in Potterston to get the part. They wouldn't close at the dinner hour the way most stores in Acorn Hill did.

She didn't know whether she could turn off water to the shower only, so she had to turn off the supply for the whole inn. At the moment, there weren't any guests in the rooms, but she couldn't leave the water off for long.

Her father's old toolbox was out in the shed where she'd last used it. She found it, but since she wasn't sure what she would need, she couldn't select just a tool or two. She lugged the heavy metal box up to the second floor along with the book of instructions.

The first step was to remove the faucet. That looked easy enough. Unfortunately nothing was ever quite as simple as the illustrations in a book suggested. The pocket knife slipped as she was trying to do the first step, and bright red blood brought her up short. She'd sliced her index finger, not seriously, but she couldn't continue bleeding all over the plumbing. She wrapped a washcloth around her finger and raced downstairs for the first-aid kit in the supply room. It was awkward trying to care for the wound with her left hand, but she finally managed to wrap a bandage around it.

Unfortunately, it soaked through almost as soon as she had it in place.

Louise's pupil was still picking out a tune. Jane decided not to interrupt, although she certainly was in need of help. Maybe Louise could go to the Potterston store after the lesson—if Jane could get the old cartridge loose. So far, she hadn't even managed to complete step one.

Much to her consternation, the Snypers came into the foyer just as she was about to go back upstairs, a clean dishcloth wrapped around her finger to absorb any blood seeping around the edges of the bandage.

"You've hurt yourself!" Isabel said.

"It's nothing," Jane said, although she was going to have to go back to the kitchen and try a larger bandage. The cloth was already spotted with blood.

"It looks serious," Isabel insisted. "Why not let me take a look at it. I took a first-aid course a few years ago."

"Thank you, but I'll be fine. I do have bad news, though. I had to turn off the water temporarily. We have a leaky shower, and I'm trying to fix it."

"Shouldn't you call a plumber?" Isabel asked with concern.

"I tried. Apparently every plumber in the county quits work at five sharp."

"I'll take a look," Vern said matter-of-factly.

How could she let a guest inspect the plumbing? How could she not?

"That's okay, I think I know how to fix it. My father left a book on home repairs."

"Let me take care of your finger," Isabel said. "Vern is a whiz with plumbing."

She could stand arguing and bleeding or let them have a go.

"The first-aid kit is in the kitchen," she said, wondering how on earth a wonderful musician like Louise could listen to such sour notes—when Jane needed her.

Isabel cleaned her cut and put on some medication, two steps Jane had omitted in her haste to get back to the leaky shower. She made a thicker bandage from two gauze pads and bound them with adhesive tape.

"You might need stitches," she cautioned.

Jane had thought of that, but there was no time now. She would show it to Alice when she got home—and what on earth was taking her so long?

By the time she got back to the leaky shower, Vern was on his hands and knees working diligently on the corroded cartridge.

"It doesn't want to come out," he admitted. "You wouldn't have a cartridge puller in the house, would you?"

"Not that I know of," Jane said. "Most of my father's tools are in that box."

"There isn't one there. Let me give your hardware store a call."

"I tried. The store is closed. But you can call him at his home. He's an old friend. I'll give you his number and you can call him from the kitchen."

The three of them paraded back down the stairs with Isabel hovering over the wounded Jane.

She sat at the table with her throbbing finger while Isabel brewed some soothing tea for both of them. She'd never felt quite so helpless. If Vern couldn't get the old shower cartridge out, what would her chances have been?

Before they'd finished a second cup of tea, Fred arrived at the house to lend Vern the necessary tool from his home toolbox. Between them they extracted the old part, then Fred went back to the store to get a replacement that, thankfully, he had in stock.

"A lot of folks in town have that kind of shower," he explained, "so I keep a few on hand."

Louise came into the kitchen, her last lesson of the day finished, and Jane let Isabel explain the plumbing crisis.

"You should have told me. I can always reschedule a lesson."

Jane only nodded. She didn't want to point out that her sister's plumbing skills were nonexistent.

Alice and Clay returned to the inn, and Jane gladly made good on her promise to lend him the car for the evening. In fact, she was feeling rather inadequate, and the kitchen was too crowded for her bruised ego. She'd had to be rescued by a guest, and not even a guest that she was especially fond of.

"I have an idea," Alice said. "Why don't I pull some frozen pizzas from the freezer? We can all have dinner together."

Alice was taking over on dinner, Louise was running back and forth from the kitchen to the shower to keep Jane apprised of the men's progress, and Isabel was being so nice that Jane didn't know what to make of her.

Isabel rinsed lettuce and tossed it in a wooden bowl as Louise prepared the dining room table. Alice called Vera to join them.

Before the pizza was done, Fred and Vern came into the kitchen to display the bad cartridge and announce that the shower was leak-free. Fred turned the water on, and Vern scrubbed up at the kitchen sink. Louise and Alice thanked them profusely.

Jane tried her best to sound grateful, but loving one's enemies was a whole lot more difficult than offering them dinner. Vern had done her a big favor, and she was indebted to him. But she couldn't forget that he and Isabel might start a bed-and-breakfast that could possibly drive Grace Chapel Inn out of business. Not only that, they were still posing as ordinary guests while they tried to learn all they could about how the Howard sisters managed theirs. They might even see the shower problem as an advantage. The inn was over one hundred years old and required constant maintenance. Their bed-and-breakfast promised to be more profitable because it was newer, and Vern could do his own repairs.

Dinner wasn't the festive event that the cookout had been, and the Humberts left soon after they'd had their pizza and salad. Vern and Isabel drifted off, and Alice took the opportunity to look at Jane's cut.

"You won't need stitches," she said, "but try to give that finger a rest. I'll change the bandage for you tomorrow."

Jane groaned but didn't protest. Caring for a finger was minor. Being appreciative for the Snypers' help was more difficult.

Life would be so simple if black was black and white was white, but gray was confusing. Alice was by nature so good that it wasn't in her to be unkind to anyone. Louise was so strong in her faith and her standards that she was able to stand up to every situation. Jane still wished that she'd never set eyes on either of the Snypers, but she didn't like the way she felt.

She had much to pray about when she would finally be alone. The Lord's command to love one's enemies seemed so difficult. She felt humiliated by the need for the Snypers' help and diminished in her own eyes by her failure to love them as she felt she ought.

Chapter Eleven

*A*lice arrived at work early on Wednesday morning. She was hoping to see Jody before they both had to begin work. So far her coworker hadn't shown her either of the articles she was writing. While they didn't have a strict deadline, the committee had hoped to bring out the first issue by the beginning of September. That meant getting the copy to the public relations department quite soon. The personnel there were already busy and needed at least two weeks to produce the finished newsletter.

Jody was one of the most conscientious young nurses on the staff, so Alice didn't doubt that she would come through on the articles. Still, it would relieve her mind to see at least one of them. Jody might be finding them more difficult to write than she'd expected. Alice felt competent to edit them for spelling, grammar and such, but it would be most unfortunate if they weren't suitable for publication. She was imagining all sorts of problems when Jody came into the staff room.

"Good morning," Alice said. "I was hoping to catch you before you went on duty."

Jody gave her a blank look, as though she didn't understand why Alice would want to see her.

She was looking different this morning, Alice noticed.

"You had your hair cut. It looks lovely," she said.

"Oh, do you think so?" She patted the blonde curls that had been styled into a very becoming halo of gold.

Jody looked different in other ways, although Alice was hard-pressed to think why. She was standing straighter, which seemed to take weight away from her middle, but that wasn't the biggest change. Her face seemed to glow, but again, it was difficult to pin down the exact change.

"Definitely," Alice said. "I was wondering whether you've finished the articles."

"Not yet. I did have a question about Dr. Jackson's interview. My aunt's friend had a heart attack, and she said her jaw hurt. I couldn't remember whether he mentioned that as one of the symptoms."

"I don't remember either. Have you played back the recording?"

"No, sorry, I just haven't had time."

"He gave us quite a bit of literature. I imagine the answer to your question must be in it. I probably should have asked more questions during the interview."

As Alice remembered it, they hadn't spent much time with him. Maybe she had been too considerate of the busy doctor's schedule.

"How is the article on diabetes coming?"

Jody blushed. Alice didn't take that as a good sign. In fact, she was beginning to feel like a teacher checking on homework.

"I'll try hard to finish them this weekend. I have both days off."

"If it's too much for you—"

"No, I promise I'll get them both done."

It was so unlike Jody not to finish something she started that Alice couldn't help wondering about the young woman's relationship with Clay. Was he spending so much time with her that she couldn't find time for the articles? Or was he just such a major distraction that she couldn't focus? Either way, she didn't begrudge Jody the excitement of getting to know a very special young man like Clay. She was still amazed that two people who barely spoke when they were introduced had formed such a promising bond so quickly. She didn't take credit for bringing them together. Clearly, the Lord was working in one of his mysterious ways with the two young people.

"We have another interview this afternoon," Alice reminded her.

Jody looked so distressed that Alice felt sorry for her.

"I'm afraid I forgot."

"Tell you what, why don't I handle it alone? You already have two articles to write. It will be good practice for me to try writing one myself. It's with an elderly woman who belongs to our church. She's ninety-seven and still lively and engaged with the world around her. I thought it might be interesting to get her ideas on staying active and healthy."

"Are you sure you don't need me?" Jody didn't quite succeed in keeping the relief out of her voice.

"Quite sure, but if it's at all possible, please finish the two articles this weekend."

Alice expected Clay to leave before then, which might give Jody more time to complete her writing.

Louise didn't see Clay when she came downstairs prepared for yet another walk with Ethel and Florence. She could hear guests in the dining room, but a quick peek showed that he wasn't among them.

"Walking again?" Jane asked when Louise went into the kitchen, where bacon and cinnamon scented the air.

Louise nodded in reply, then breathed deeply and smiled. She especially enjoyed the heavenly aromas that permeated the air while Jane was working her magic. This morning her sister had outdone herself with homemade cinnamon rolls and baked eggs made from a recipe she'd modified to give it her special touch. Jane's secret ingredient was very finely shredded red onion along with Gruyère cheese and a generous measure of crisp minced bacon. They had to be baked in a water bath until set, and Jane was hovering over the oven, waiting to test them.

She'd put special effort into the fruit cups too. Several extra ones were sitting on the counter, and Louise saw that they contained halved green grapes, fresh pineapple, strawberries and bananas topped with yogurt dressing and shredded coconut. As if that weren't enough, she had a partial pitcher of freshly squeezed orange juice waiting for latecomers and a basket of whole wheat rolls for anyone who might want to pass up the luscious, frosted cinnamon buns.

"You've really outdone yourself this morning," Louise said. "You must have been up before dawn to let the rolls rise."

"To tell the truth, I didn't sleep very well," Jane admitted as she pulled the pan of baked eggs out of the oven. "You can help me by putting just a little cream sauce and a shake of paprika on each serving."

"Is something wrong?" her sister asked as she followed Jane's instructions.

"No—yes." Jane softly laughed at herself and lowered her voice to a whisper. "I just felt bad about not thanking Vern more than I did."

"I was sure you had."

"I said the words, but I resented being helped by a person who came here under false pretenses. They mean to put us out of business, you know."

"No, I don't know that," Louise said in a low voice. "I'm confident that Grace Chapel Inn fills a need in the community. We don't know that it won't survive competition from a second bed-and-breakfast—if they even go through with it."

"You're right, of course," Jane agreed. "I guess an especially nice breakfast is my way of compensating. You can serve these now if you wouldn't mind."

Louise carried food to the table, then had time to enjoy Jane's egg dish herself before she was scheduled to walk again. Yesterday had gone fairly well, but she knew it was because Clay had joined them. Since he hadn't come down for breakfast yet, she didn't really expect him to walk with them today.

Florence came to the inn before Ethel got there.

"I was so eager for our outing that I left the car in the Chapel parking lot and decided to walk over," she said, looking especially smart in a new navy and white striped top and crisp white pants.

Louise noticed that she had a different hat too, a smaller, jauntier straw one.

"Has Clay had his breakfast?" she asked, trying to sound casual.

"No, we haven't seen him yet this morning," Louise said.

"I imagine we moved a bit too slowly for him." Florence didn't quite manage to hide her disappointment. "Well, Ethel isn't here yet, so perhaps he'll still join us."

"Perhaps," Louise agreed absentmindedly, trying to think of all the things she wanted to accomplish that day.

She definitely needed to make a trip to the music store in Potterston to look over some new compositions that her students might be able to use in the fall. Although she didn't change the basic pieces from year to year, she did like to assign some modern music to her older students. It went a long way toward holding their interest.

A trip to the shoe store was in order too. Ethel and Florence's brand new athletic shoes had inspired her to take a long look at her own, and they were definitely too shabby and worn for long walks. She was a great believer in foot health. Maybe she would suggest that Alice do a wellness article on it.

"Good morning, everyone," Ethel trilled as she sailed into the kitchen. "I have exciting news. Viola is going to join us this morning. I told her what a lovely walk we had yesterday with Clay, and she should be here any minute."

"I don't think he's coming with us this morning," Florence said in the tone of a person delivering bad news.

"Well, we'll see." Ethel wasn't about to accept Florence's word for it.

Louise offered to make tea for the walkers because Jane was busy with their guests in the dining room. They declined, and only moments later Viola Reed, the owner of Acorn Hill's only bookstore, came into the kitchen.

"Good morning, everyone," she said cheerfully. "I've decided to give up my slothful ways and join you on the open road."

Louise was a bit surprised to see her wearing a pair of somewhat snug pink walking shorts and an oversized blouse that hung to midthigh. Her walking shoes were almost as scuffed as Louise's. She was around Louise's age with very short steel-gray hair and prominent brown eyes, and the group promised to be livelier with her presence.

After a minute or two of chatting, Viola made it clear that she knew a few things about the young man who was staying at the inn.

"Imagine, walking all the way from Nebraska," she said with wonderment. "Do you think he'll join us this morning?"

"It doesn't appear so," Louise said, hating to be the one to give her bad news.

"Well, no matter." Viola sounded disappointed but rallied quickly. "This is such a good idea. The only exercise I get is taking care of my cats. It's not as if I had dogs that need to be walked every day."

"Am I too late?"

Ethel squealed, Florence purred and Viola gawked at the very tall young man who came into the kitchen.

"Clay, this is—" Florence began.

"Yes, I've met Ms. Reed," he said. "I can't believe what a good collection of Mark Twain books she has in her store."

"I convinced Clay to try Dickens' *Great Expectations*," she said. "How are you finding it?"

"I've only just started, but I'm sure I'll enjoy it."

"So you are joining us this morning," Ethel said. "I'm so pleased."

"My pleasure, Miss Ethel," he said with a grin.

Louise was sure he had to be one of the sweetest young men on the planet.

The five of them filed out of the inn with minor jockeying for position. Florence immediately occupied one side of Clay, although he didn't offer his arm. Poor Ethel was squeezed out when Viola resumed the book conversation that they'd apparently begun when he visited her shop.

"I haven't had much call for Faulkner or Steinbeck," Viola said, "but now that I've talked to you, I'm considering a special display. I wonder if you've ever read Thomas Hardy. His novels are gloomy, I suppose, but his insights into the human condition are still revealing today."

"I have a surprise for all of you after our walk," Florence said, not to be upstaged by the bookstore owner.

"I've never been a fan of surprise endings," Viola said, apparently too wrapped up in her subject to pay attention to Florence. "If an author is a master writer, the plot will evolve spontaneously from the nature of the characters."

"Sometimes it's fun to be fooled, though," Clay said, taking an enthusiastic part in the discussion.

"I saw this movie—I forget the name," Florence said, "but it was about smoking out people who weren't really human. I was certainly surprised when the man hunting them down was some kind of robot himself. Of course, science fiction isn't at all my cup of tea, but my husband likes to rent a DVD from time to time. Usually I read while he's watching. I always say that you can learn a lot more from a good book."

"Yes, you certainly can," Clay said politely.

Ethel was lagging behind without Clay's friendly arm to propel her forward. Louise stayed with her, glad that she'd resisted the temptation to skip the walk today. She wouldn't like to have her aunt trailing behind all by herself.

Louise would have liked to walk faster, but at least Ethel wasn't a distraction today. She could walk and think at the same time, and there was much to occupy her thoughts. Although she'd tried to reassure Jane that Grace Chapel Inn could survive competition from a second bed-and-breakfast, she knew that the basis of their success was filling most of the guest rooms most of the time. They could ride out a few slow days now and then, as they had with the recent cancellations, but a choice of places to stay in Acorn Hill could leave them in financial trouble.

Without the income from the bed-and-breakfast, they might have to sell their father's house. The thought greatly saddened her. She and Alice had the means to continue living together in Acorn Hill, but Jane was too young for retirement. She might have to find a chef's job somewhere else, since the town didn't have a crying need for a chef with her culinary skills.

"They're getting ahead of us," Ethel said, interrupting Louise's thoughts. "Let's step it up a little."

Louise realized that her gloomy thoughts had slowed her down even more than keeping pace with her aunt. She gladly started moving a little faster.

This morning Florence's route took them around the circumference of the town, then down Village Road to the

Dairyland gas and convenience store. They turned around there, and Louise wanted to hug Clay when he made a special point of asking Ethel to walk with him. She happily trotted along on his arm while Florence staked out his other side. Viola dropped back beside Louise.

"I have to confess," Viola said, "I'm really not in shape for this. Usually the farthest I walk is from my house to the store, and I take the car when I have something to carry. I thought I'd walk with your club once just for fun, but I can see that I need to become a regular."

"I have to give Florence and Ethel credit," Louise said. "It was their idea. I walk on my own whenever I have time, but some weeks I'm just too busy. Having a set time early in the morning works well for me."

"Yes, it's the one time of day when I don't have an excuse not to do it," Viola said. "But I can tell already that I have to invest in a better pair of shoes. I've had these so long that I can't remember when I bought them. They seem to have gotten tighter. Do you suppose shoes shrink when you don't wear them for a long time?"

"I've heard that your feet do change size sometimes even when you're an adult, but that could be hearsay," Louise said.

"More likely mine have just gotten fatter," Viola said laughing. "I had quite a time finding some shorts that fit in my wardrobe. Luckily I have this big shirt to cover as much of me as possible. I usually only wear it when I'm housecleaning."

"It works well," Louise said politely.

"It covers me like a tent!" Viola laughed so loudly that the others looked back over their shoulders.

"Just girl talk," Louise assured them.

"Between you and me," Viola said in a confidential voice, "I have noticed that the waistbands on some of my favorite skirts are pinching a bit. And I had to take off a blouse the other morning because it strained between the buttons. Do you think I look heavier?"

It was a question no friend should answer with yes. Louise didn't.

"Of course, you're too kind to tell me," Viola said cheerfully. "Anyway, a daily walk may be just what I need. I never was very good about diets and calorie-counting and such, but I guess I could give up desserts for a while. And snacks. I do love a plate of cheese and crackers before bed. Or a cup of hot chocolate with marshmallows and a piece of nice, buttery Scotch shortbread in the winter. Oh dear, I guess I deserve putting on a few pounds."

"It's hard not to," Louise agreed.

"You must have iron willpower, not to swell up like a balloon on Jane's delicious cooking," Viola mused, slowing up a little as she talked.

"The others are getting ahead of us," Louise pointed out.

In fact, Ethel and Florence were moving along quite briskly, keeping up with what was a leisurely pace for Clay. They were headed back down Hill Street when Florence stopped and waved one arm like a traffic warden.

"Now for my surprise," she said when Louise and Viola caught up. "I made arrangements for the Coffee Shop to prepare a family-style breakfast for us after our walk. I want all of you to join me, my treat. Everything should be ready for us."

"It's awfully nice of you, Florence, but I had breakfast before I left," Louise said in an attempt to decline politely.

"Then come have coffee with us. I won't hear of you passing up my treat," she said.

"Well, I suppose coffee would be fine."

The Coffee Shop was busy with the breakfast crowd, but Hope Collins, the restaurant's popular waitress, greeted them and led them to the reserved table.

"I didn't know what you would want, so I ordered an assortment to pass around," Florence said. "Now, would you like coffee or tea? You can just leave the pots on the table, thank you, Hope, and I'll pour."

Louise was eager to get on with her day, but she realized that fellowship was a big part of the walking club. She didn't see how she could join them each and every morning, but she couldn't deny that the potential benefits for all of the women made it worth an effort.

"I'm afraid I'll have to eat and run," Viola said regretfully. "I have to clean up before I open my store."

"That's why I arranged to have everything ready for us," Florence said with satisfaction.

The Coffee Shop was known for large portions of favorite dishes, and they'd outdone themselves for the walkers.

"If anyone would like something else, I'll be glad to get it for you," Hope said.

There were no takers, understandably since the table was crowded with more food than double their number could eat. Louise's first reaction was that a meal like this would more than undo any good effects from the rather short walk. Her second thought was that it was a terrible waste because there was no way five people could eat so much.

Clay looked troubled.

"This is so much food for five people, Mrs. Simpson," he said in a low voice, as though talking to himself.

Florence heard him and took his words as a compliment. "I wanted to do something special to reward my walking friends."

Louise was afraid he hadn't meant it as a positive comment. She read the disapproval in his face. It almost seemed to say that waste was inexcusable.

Suspecting that Florence's treat was meant in part to have Clay think well of her, and knowing that she would be hurt if anyone rejected her hospitality, Louise took a small piece of corn bread and one piece of bacon. She wasn't alone. Perhaps it was the good effect of the morning walk, but all seemed to be sparing in what they put on their plates. Viola took a small portion of eggs and a single sausage. Ethel passed up the eggs and meat in favor of a bagel drizzled with honey, and Clay ate sparingly of the protein dishes.

Florence initially took something of almost every dish until her plate was heaped to capacity, but after a few bites, she seemed to realize that she was alone in taking so much. When the breakfast ended, her plate was still more than half full.

"Would you like to take the leftovers home?" Hope offered with her usual quiet efficiency.

"No, I don't think so," Florence said.

"My neighbor broke her ankle last week and hasn't been able to get out to shop," Viola said. "I think she might appreciate a nice breakfast."

"What a good idea!" Florence said. "We have a shut-in from our church who lives just a block away. I know she might enjoy some of the soft foods, especially some eggs and biscuits. I can drop it off on my way home."

Clay was smiling for the first time since they'd entered the Coffee Shop. He exchanged a look with Louise, and she smiled at him.

What an extraordinary young man he was! By eating moderately himself, he'd inspired the three women to think of the needs of others. And he'd done it without criticizing, cajoling or even suggesting.

⌒

Alice couldn't believe the little flutter in her stomach. She was actually nervous about interviewing Maud Schoonamaker, a Chapel member she'd known since childhood. What was it about the prospect of doing an article about her that was intimidating?

She arrived at Maud's cozy little cottage promptly at four with her recorder and a list of questions. The interview was sure to be interesting. Maud had a quick wit and a loving nature, but she wasn't shy about letting people know what she was thinking.

At ninety-seven she was the oldest member of Grace Chapel still living alone in her own home. Members of the congregation checked on her regularly, but she resisted all suggestions that she move to an assisted-living facility. Her husband had passed on many years before, and her only son had retired to Florida. In spite of his repeated invitations to join him there, she preferred life in Acorn Hill. Alice could understand her decision, but, like many others in town, she worried about her.

"Come in, Alice," Maud said when she opened the screen door.

"How are you, Maud?"

She stepped directly into the small living room, one that always reminded her of a child's playhouse. The hardwood flooring gleamed from many years of polishing, and the room was furnished with a single reclining chair, two period rockers, including quite an old platform one with carved armrests and deep burgundy upholstery. A single Queen Anne–style occasional table with one small drawer sat beside the recliner, and a rather plain oak stand held a spider plant that drooped down to the floor. A pale watercolor landscape hung on one wall, and several framed family photos graced another. The ceiling was lower than most, which added to the dollhouse atmosphere.

"I get by. I found this bowl that I used to use for my gelatin salad," Maud said, holding out a pretty transfer-printed bowl with a lovely rose design. "I want you and your sisters to have it."

Maud had been giving away her possessions for as long as Alice could remember. Certainly her cupboards must be nearly empty by now. Everyone who visited her was presented with a keepsake sooner or later, and most, like Alice, felt awkward accepting it.

"Don't you think your son or one of your granddaughters would like it?" Alice asked.

"No, they run a mile when I try giving them any more of my old stuff. I want you to have it."

"Thank you, Maud. I'm sure we'll enjoy using it."

"I have water on for tea, if you don't mind sitting in the kitchen."

"Not at all."

Maud was taller than average and only slightly stooped by age. Some time ago she'd taken to wearing wigs, claiming that they kept her head warm. They were her only vanity, and she had a collection in a variety of colors. Today she was wearing a dark auburn one that was nicely bobbed. It emphasized her sunken cheeks and deeply incised wrinkles, but she was saved from looking grotesque by her lively personality.

"I hope you don't mind store-bought cookies. I don't have much appetite these days, and I can't remember when I last baked."

Alice assured her that the vanilla wafers Maud shook out from a box were fine.

"What was it you wanted to ask me?" Maud asked as she poured tea into two delicate gold-rimmed cups.

"I'm in charge of a wellness newsletter for the hospital staff," Alice explained. "I guess what everyone would most like to know is—"

"How I got to be so old. People ask me that a lot. Seem to think I've discovered the fountain of youth, but I tell you, getting old isn't for sissies. It's hard work, plain and simple."

She pointed at an exercise bike that sat in one corner of the kitchen in front of a shelf holding a small television.

"I'm on that contraption every day, seven days a week."

"Would you mind if I record what you say?" Alice asked.

"If you like, but I don't have any secrets to tell."

Alice flipped on the recorder and sipped her tea. She was beginning to feel that she was intruding on Maud's privacy.

Thinking through her list of questions, she didn't know where to start.

"Did your parents or grandparents live as long as you?" she eventually asked, wondering if she was being tactful enough.

"If you mean, do I have good genes, I guess I must have gotten some. My grandfather lived to eighty-six, but my father and uncle went in their seventies. My mother was taken at ninety-two, but my little sister didn't live to see seventy."

Her face took on a faraway look as she remembered all her lost loved ones. Alice was hesitant about going on, but Maud took the initiative.

"I always like to sleep eight hours a night," she said pushing the plate of vanilla wafers across the checkered oilcloth on her table. "These days I nap a bit too, maybe twenty minutes after lunch. I smile a lot, even when I'm alone, and I still enjoy a good laugh from time to time. I do crosswords, although it takes me longer than it used to. I have to use a magnifying glass to see the tiny print. My, all that makes my days seem dull, but I manage to eke out a little fun now and again, especially when friends like you drop in."

"You have many friends, Maud."

"Your little sister is a sweetheart. Brings me plates of homemade cookies. Don't tell her, but I put them in the freezer to save for company. I don't have much of a sweet tooth these days."

"It's our secret," Alice said, knowing that Maud didn't want Jane's visits to stop.

"There you have it."

What Alice didn't have was enough to write an article. She tried to think of Carlene's advice, but she felt as though she'd hit a wall.

"Of course, you can figure out the real secret for yourself," Maud said with a sly smile.

"Your faith." Alice suddenly realized that this was the core of Maud's being.

"I try to keep the faith every day. I talk to the Lord, and I know that when it's my time to go, He'll call me to His heavenly kingdom. It's what I learned in Sunday school all those years ago, and nothing's changed just because I've got a lot of mileage on me."

Alice smiled, feeling the warmth that flowed from the fragile older woman.

"One other thing, I don't think people should be all wrapped up in themselves. A woman who doesn't care about other folks is never going to be at peace with herself. That's what I think anyway. When I read my Bible—thanks to Rev. Thompson I have one with big letters I can see without my magnifying glass—that's the message I find. It distresses me that I can't do much for others anymore, but I can pray for them. I can and I do. Well, I don't know what you can put in your article about wellness. My body feels like a reed in a high wind these days, but the Lord hasn't seen fit to call me home yet. When He does, I'm ready."

Maud had found comfort in a spiritual resource that provided aid beyond the reach of medical practice.

Alice could feel tears building up. She reached in her uniform pocket for a tissue, intending to mask them with a sneeze. Then she looked into Maud's eyes and realized that crying tears of joy with a friend wasn't something that needed to be hidden. She gently took the elderly woman in her arms, and there was no need to say anything.

Chapter Twelve

*J*ane wasn't at all sure how to handle the problem of the double-booked room for Friday night. In fact, she wasn't even sure that Clay wanted to stay that night. If he did, where could she put him?

She'd hoped to sound him out about his plans at breakfast Thursday, but she was so busy with a new recipe that he'd come and gone before she had a chance.

At least the ladies of the walking club would be delighted. He'd once again decided to join them. Their numbers were swelling according to Ethel, who'd popped into the kitchen while Louise was having a quick bowl of cereal. Viola had joined them yesterday, and today Carlene Moss joined them again. Jane thought that their outings were beginning to sound like fun. Louise agreed, even though she wasn't sure that their slow pace provided maximum benefit. Nevertheless, according to her, they did seem to be moving faster than they had the first day. She was hopeful that they would step it up as they got used to walking.

Jane might have been tempted to join them herself for the companionship, but, of course, she was much too busy with the guests' breakfasts to leave first thing in the morning.

"That was a lovely omelet," Isabel said, poking her head into the kitchen after finishing breakfast. "Do you have a regular rotation of entrées, or do you just fix whatever strikes your fancy?"

"I plan by the week," Jane said, making a show of cleaning off the stove top.

How much more help did the Snypers expect to get from her? If it were her decision alone, she would confront them. Maybe if Jane's resentment was made known, they would have the grace to leave.

Or maybe not. Florence's latest report via her real estate agent's connection was that the Snypers had made an offer on the property they wanted. Apparently it was too low, so the question was, would they up the amount they were willing to pay and actually go into competition with Grace Chapel Inn?

"I didn't see your sister Louise this morning. She usually helps you with breakfast, doesn't she?" Isabel was looking smart in a beige linen pantsuit with a cocoa-brown shell, the kind of outfit that was appropriate for a business meeting.

"Louise helps when she can, but our aunt has convinced her to join a walking club in the morning."

"What a wonderful idea. I keep telling Vern that we really should get more exercise. Can I help you clear the table since you're here all alone?"

"Thank you, but I can manage. I'm not quite ready to deal with the dishes. I have to unload the dishwasher first."

"Yes, I imagine you have a certain routine that works best for you. You certainly seem to be well organized. Do you rely on charts and worksheets, or does it just come naturally to you?"

"A combination, I suppose."

"Acorn Hill is such a charming little town," Isabel said. "I feel safe walking at any time of day or night. You certainly can't say that about large cities. I imagine your insurance rates are lower here, given that there's practically no crime."

"Louise takes care of the financial arrangements," Jane said. "I've no idea how rates compare to other places."

"Of course, you're such a wizard in the kitchen. It would be a waste of your talent to concern yourself with business details like that."

Jane felt a response on the tip of her tongue, but nothing would be gained by explaining how the three of them worked together on most things that had to do with the inn. All their important decisions were made as a group.

Isabel lingered for a while longer, but Jane turned the conversation to a topic that didn't interest the guest in the least—the weather.

"Well, if you're sure I can't help you, I'll be on my way," Isabel said after halfheartedly agreeing that the summer was unseasonably dry.

"Have a nice day," Jane said trying to sound more cheerful than she felt.

Alice couldn't get Maud out of her mind as she went about her duties that morning. Although she was on the run most of the time, she still felt touched by her elderly friend's faith. Maud had put her life in the Lord's hands. It gave her a serenity not often seen in people of any age.

Alice was working with surgical patients who'd passed the crisis point and were, for the most part, eager to get back to their normal lives. Although a few were quite demanding, Alice was sympathetic. Once a person started to feel better, the hospital routine could be irksome.

She hadn't substituted on this floor for several months, but even with her help, they were shorthanded. Fortunately the regular staff included some top-notch nurses, including

Rick, a young man who was more than competent and exceptionally compassionate. Several patients made a point of telling her how much they appreciated him. In fact, he reminded her a little of Clay. He had a gift for making people feel better about themselves.

Her lunch break gave her a little time to think about the interview with Maud. She was stymied about how to start the article. In fact, she didn't have a clue how to write any part of it. The elderly woman had deep spiritual resources, but how did they fit in with the aims of the wellness newsletter? Longevity was such a complicated subject. No doubt genes played a crucial part, as did lifestyle, but, in addition, Maud had a tranquil spirit that defined her. What part did her faith play? How could Alice leave that out of the article and still be true to her subject? In fact, she couldn't, but Maud's story didn't exactly fit the guidelines that the committee had set up for the newsletter.

She wished that she had her father's gift for touching people at their very core with words. Daniel Howard called on his deep faith in writing sermons that motivated people toward a more spiritual life.

Alice expressed her faith through service to others. She knew how to speak kindly, to reassure and bring comfort, but writing an article was something new. Where would she get the words she needed?

Maybe she'd made a mistake in not taking Jody with her. She could play the recording for her, but it wasn't the same as seeing and hearing Maud at the same time. Nor could she pile more work on her. If Jody finished the two articles as promised, it would be a great relief. There was no way Alice could ask her to do a third.

She returned after lunch to find a problem with one of her patients. An elderly man who was recovering from hip replacement surgery was refusing to go to his therapy session. The licensed practical nurse who was supposed to take him there in a wheelchair had given up, and the floor supervisor had given him a stern talk about what needed to happen before he could go home.

"What's up?" Rick asked, just returning from lunch himself. He was a rather slight, dark-haired man in his midthirties, but his small stature belied his strength. He was often called upon when a patient had to be lifted.

The supervisor explained the problem, and Rick hurried into the patient's room. A few minutes later he emerged pushing him in the wheelchair. There was no protest when Rick turned the chair over to the LPN.

"Thank you, Rick," the supervisor said when the patient was on his way to therapy. "You really have a gift for working with difficult people."

"I just listen to their stories," he said with a modest smile, going on to his next responsibility.

His words stuck with Alice for the rest of her shift. People loved to tell stories even more than they liked to hear them. Was there something here that could help her with Maud's story? She was too busy to think it through, but she felt the beginning of an idea. She only hoped it would develop into an article she could use.

She was still debating with herself about the best way to tell Maud's story as she walked out to her car. When she opened the door, the heat inside was stifling. Even with the cardboard sun shield she'd put on the front window, the interior had heated up to an almost unbearable temperature.

Alice opened the car doors to let the hot air escape for a few minutes before she got inside. She wasn't alone in the parking lot. A number of people were making their way to their vehicles at the end of their workday. Several waved at Alice, including a helmeted motorcycle rider whom she recognized as Rick, the nurse she'd worked with today. Most were too intent on getting home to stop and visit, but one figure in a cheerful rose-colored uniform veered directly toward her.

"Jody," she called out. "Do you need a ride home?"

"No, I have my mother's car—well, actually it's half mine. We decided we really didn't need two cars plus the pickup my dad drives, not that he's home much with his job."

"I'm just letting mine cool down a bit before I get inside."

"Good idea. It's really hot today."

Jody lingered, and Alice sensed that she had more on her mind than the heat wave.

"I'm sorry about the articles. I promise I'll finish both of them this weekend."

Alice didn't doubt it, since Jody had already promised to do so.

"That will be soon enough. I'm a bit stymied myself about the one I'm writing about longevity. I had a wonderful interview, but I'm afraid I won't be able to do it justice."

Jody was squinting in the bright sun, so it was hard to read her face. Still, Alice felt sure that she wanted to talk about something that was important to her.

"I don't know what to do," she said sounding close to tears.

"Can I help?" Alice asked, motioning for the young nurse to sit in her car while she went around to the other side.

"No one can," Jody said miserably. "All my life I've been afraid that I would never meet someone to love, someone who loves me too. Now I have, and it's just terrible."

Alice listened without making any comments. She sensed that no amount of advice would help Jody as much as just hearing her out.

"It's Clay," she said. "He's going to leave, you know. He's promised to give talks along the way, and he's already behind schedule. I just don't know what I'll do when he goes. My mother says it's only a crush, that I'll meet other fellows. But it's not."

Oh dear, Alice thought. *I never intended for this to happen.*

"I haven't had a lot of boyfriends like some of my friends," Jody went on. "I always dreamed of meeting someone who would be my soul mate, and I think I have. But having him leave so soon is a nightmare. I don't know what to do. I don't think there is anything I can do. He'll go, and I'll never see him again."

Her eyes sparkled with tears, but Alice was at a loss as to how to comfort her. Clay would leave. He was too committed to his cause to give it up now. Jody would miss him, maybe for a long time. It was a distressing situation, and her sympathy went out to her young friend.

"He cares about me just the way I am. My mother is always telling me to lose weight or have my nails done or change my hairstyle. She says you have to package yourself, but I don't believe her anymore. Clay doesn't want to change me. He liked my hair the way it was, but he likes it this way too. He looks past things like that. He likes me for who I am."

"I'm sure he does. You're a wonderful person, and he can see that."

"Maybe, but I'm sure he can find someone better." She sniffled and dug in her purse for a tissue.

"Don't feel that way, Jody. You're a lovely young woman. Any man would be privileged to know you."

"Thank you, but it doesn't make me feel any better."

"No, I suppose not," Alice said gently, "but you do have one very important thing in common with Clay."

"What's that?" She blotted her eyes on a fresh tissue.

"You both care very much about other people. I've seen you at work, and nursing is much more than just a job to you. Clay must see how committed you are, and service to others is something he values very highly from all that I've seen. Do you know that he's been walking every morning with some of the older women in Acorn Hill? They adore him, and he's encouraging them to walk for wellness. Not many young men would do something like that."

"He is special, isn't he? I'm going to miss him horribly."

Alice wanted to assure her that their friendship would continue, but she didn't feel that she had a right to speculate that way. Now that she thought about it, she was going to miss him too in her own way. He seemed to spread sunshine wherever he went.

"Thank you for listening, Alice. I'd better go now. I don't know whether I'll see Clay this evening, but I want to shower and change just in case. I guess my mother isn't all wrong. It does give a person confidence to look as good as possible."

Alice watched Jody walk to her car, remembering a time when she had been in love and threatened with separation. She'd come close to marrying Mark Graves in their college days, and even now she had an occasional twinge of regret. True, they'd renewed their friendship in recent times, but they couldn't get back the years of separation. Even now, her commitment to her job and to her sisters conflicted with his job as head vet at the Philadelphia Zoo.

She smiled at her own musing. There was nothing she regretted about her life, especially not her commitment to the Lord. It was only recently that Mark had come to know their Savior. What they had now was very special to both of them, but it was different from the first enchantment of youthful love.

She drove home, too distracted by Jody's unhappiness to give Maud's interview more thought for the present.

Jane was trying to think of a tactful way to learn whether Clay wanted to stay longer. Of course, she could just tell him that his room wouldn't be available tomorrow night, but he'd been so good to Ethel and her group that she didn't have the heart to put him out. She thought of alternatives. Possibly he could sleep in the library. Or maybe a better idea was to set up a cot in the sunroom off the parlor. It was a small but pleasant space outfitted with wicker furniture and used only in warm weather since it was unheated. Fortunately Louise didn't have lessons on Saturday, so he wouldn't be disturbed by her pupils.

But perhaps she might be worrying for nothing. There was always the possibility that he planned to leave and wouldn't need accommodations for Friday.

"Hello," he said coming into the kitchen just as Jane finished eating a luncheon salad by herself. "Hope I'm not interrupting."

"Not at all. I'm finished. Alice is working, and Louise went to Potterston to have lunch with a friend. Can I fix you something?"

"No, I ate at the Coffee Shop, but thank you anyway. Is there anything I can do for you this afternoon? Sweeping, mowing, weeding, polishing—I'm a whiz at taking out garbage and doing laundry."

"I can't ask you to do any of that," Jane said, laughing at his extraordinary eagerness.

"Ask me to do something, please! I'm too hyper to settle down, for some reason." He cruised around the kitchen as though looking for something he could remedy.

"Well, there is one thing, but I'm not sure it's fair to ask you." Jane could see that Clay really needed a task.

"I can always say no," he said with a teasing grin.

"How do you feel about windows?"

"Windows to the sky? Windows to the soul?"

"Just plain windows. I've been putting it off and putting it off, but the inside of all the panes needs cleaning. We have the outside done by a professional as a rule. If you did all the windows on the back porch, it would be wonderful."

"Lead me to your vinegar and rags."

"Oh, I have a spray bottle of blue stuff that works really well."

He hesitated when she took it out from under the sink and offered it to him.

"We always use vinegar at our house," he said. "If you have an empty spray bottle, I can mix it up. It's simple, really, two ounces of vinegar in a quart of water. My family is into green cleaning."

"Green as in environmental?" Jane asked as she handed over a roll of paper toweling.

"Yes, I don't know all my mother's recipes for environmentally friendly cleaners, but I know whatever she uses has to be biodegradable, chlorine-free and phosphate-free. Oh yeah, she likes things unscented too. Do you have any rags?" He handed back the paper towels.

Jane smiled, knowing his requests were totally reasonable. She tried to think green in the products she used, but sometimes she was tempted to go with the quickest way, not the method that was best for the earth. At least she had an empty spray bottle, plenty of vinegar and an ample supply of cloths that he could use.

"I can give you some other earth-friendly tips, if you wouldn't mind," he said, spraying the window next to the door and beginning to polish it. "My parents are fanatics. Did you know that it takes a thousand years to totally break down a plastic bag, the common kind you get at the grocery store?"

"The supermarket in Potterston has a bin to recycle them, but it never seems very full. I have to confess, I often intend to take ours but forget."

"If you used your own fabric bags instead, you could save hundreds of plastic ones over the years. I read on the Internet that a group called Earth Share figured out that bringing your own fabric bags could amount to a savings of eleven barrels of oil in five years, what it takes to make the plastic ones. That's a pretty impressive saving, especially if enough people get behind it."

"That is amazing, a little thing like a plastic bag can add up that much," she mused.

"Sooner or later, we'll all have to use more elbow grease and fewer chemicals." He polished so hard that the window glass squeaked.

"I'm sure you're right. And I really appreciate your help," she said.

An hour or so later he'd completed all the windows that Jane had designated.

"Do you want me to do the dining room?" he asked, returning with an empty spray bottle and a big pile of soiled rags.

"You've done more than enough for one day," Jane said. "Thank you so much. Now, how about a glass of lemonade. I just made up a pitcher with fresh lemons."

"You know," he said after settling himself at the kitchen table and downing half a glass of the refreshing beverage, "you could save a lot of energy if you switched all your bulbs to CFLs."

"CFLs?"

"Compact fluorescent lamps. They're more expensive than incandescent bulbs, but they sometimes last as long as thirteen regular bulbs. Not only that, they use seventy-five percent less energy. With incandescent bulbs, ninety percent of the energy goes to generating heat, not light."

"Actually, I've been replacing the bulbs in the inn with fluorescents as they burn out. I have some in the storage room. The trouble is, there are some that I can't reach myself even with a ladder. The ones over the upper landing and in the foyer. I'll have to wait until we have a workman to do some other job."

"No need to wait," he said eagerly. "If you have a stepladder, I should be able to reach them."

"Clay, you're a guest! I can't ask you to do that kind of job."

"I don't remember you asking. Let's just say it would please me immensely if I could leave the inn just a little bit more environmentally friendly. Where do you keep the ladder?"

"Outside in the gardening shed, but I'm not sure I should let you climb so high."

"Tell you what, if I fall and break something, you can wait on me hand and foot until I can walk again," he joked.

Here was her chance to ask when he intended to resume his walk to New York, but she hesitated. He was such a wonderful guest that she really didn't want him to go yet. What other young man would walk for the sake of a group of older women? He'd been so courtly with Ethel that she glowed in his presence. Jane was enjoying his company even though she felt a bit uncomfortable letting him do an unpopular job like window washing.

There seemed to be no stopping him though. He insisted on changing bulbs for her, following her to the shed and carrying back the paint-spattered ladder she'd used in decorating all the bedrooms.

When Clay had replaced the several old-style bulbs with softly glowing fluorescents, Jane stood back and tried to decide whether she liked the different type of light. Her artist's eye was actually quite pleased. She liked the diffused effect, and the foyer and landing were just as well lit as before.

After he had finished, he carried the ladder back to the shed, leaving Jane to stand admiring his work.

Her first instinct was to offer him pay for the jobs he'd done, but then it occurred to her that there was a reward he would appreciate much more.

"I'm not going anywhere today. Would you like to use my car again?"

"Are you sure?" he asked hopefully.

"Yes, keep it as long as you like. I won't be going out this evening either."

"You're a doll!" He planted a kiss on her forehead and bounded up the stairs. "I'll just clean up and go."

"You know where the keys are," she called after him, rewarded by the expression of sheer delight on his face, as well as by the young man's gentle manifestation of gratitude.

Alice came home feeling rather hot and drained.

"How was your day?" Jane asked as she went into the kitchen.

"Long."

Jane gave her a puzzled look, but Alice didn't feel upbeat enough to explain.

"Guess what Clay did for me," Jane said enthusiastically, then went on to tell how helpful he'd been.

"That's nice," Alice agreed, "but he didn't do much for my day. Perhaps I never should have introduced him to Jody."

"Oh dear," Jane said.

"Oh dear, indeed. I'm afraid she'll be brokenhearted when he leaves. I never intended to play Cupid. I only thought the cookout would be more fun if he had someone his own age to talk to."

"Poor Jody," Jane said. "I'm afraid women of all ages are quite taken with him. I think Aunt Ethel and Florence will cry when he leaves. He's been so sweet to them, walking with their club. I'll miss him too. He's renewed my faith in what we're doing here. We may get a few undesirable guests like the Snypers, but getting to know Clay more than makes up for it."

"Yes, sometimes he reminds me of Mark when we were both young," Alice reminisced. "Not that he looks anything like him, but they're both so considerate and unselfish. Do you know how much longer he's staying?"

"I intended to ask," Jane said, looking a bit uncomfortable. "We have reservations for his room tomorrow night. Maybe I didn't pin him down because I really don't want him to go."

"You have to give him some notice if the room is taken," Alice said.

"Yes, I know, but maybe I can get him a place to stay in Potterston."

"That's a possibility," Alice conceded, "but we still should know his plans. As far as I can tell by watching him walk, his blisters have healed. I'm afraid that the longer he stays, the harder it will be for Jody to say good-bye."

"Yes, that's the sad part, but I guess there's nothing we can do."

Alice shook her head. "I'm afraid you are right. I think it's out of our hands."

Jane looked sad. "As for affairs of the heart, we can't interfere in his plans. Clay and Jody are both adults. They'll have to work it out themselves."

Chapter Thirteen

*J*ane finished whipping up eggs, then stirred in minced onions and thinly sliced smoked salmon. Next she checked the cranberry-walnut coffee cake in the oven. She was in the midst of making breakfast for seven guests.

"Good morning, Jane," said Louise, entering the kitchen. "What can I do to help?"

"Good morning. You could pour the juice, I guess. It's the white grape in the fridge."

"Something smells good," Louise said as she looked for the juice.

"Oh, my coffee cake!"

Jane rushed to the oven. "Dear, it got a little dark around the edges."

"It's not bad. If I trim the edges just a little, it will be fine," her sister said optimistically.

"I guess. I'll make some toast as an alternative. There's someone coming down the stairs. Take a peek and see who it is, would you?"

"The Snypers," Louise reported.

"I hope they don't have any questions before breakfast."

Jane reached for a wooden spoon. The stoneware bowl with the eggs was in the way so she grabbed it with one hand to move it when the unthinkable happened. It slipped from her fingers and crashed to the floor. The bowl smashed into fragments and egg splattered in all directions.

"Oh no!" She looked from the yellow mess on the black-and-white checkered floor to the bottoms of her jeans, which hadn't escaped the spill.

"I'll get the mop and pail," Louise quickly offered.

"Oh darn! I'll have to start over from scratch."

"I'll pour the guests' juice and tell them there will be a delay."

"It shouldn't take too long." Jane looked over at the stove, her way blocked by the slippery eggs on the floor.

"Good morning!"

Florence walked into the kitchen before they could warn her off, her clean walking shoe landing on a blob of egg.

"Careful, Florence, we've just had a little accident."

"So you have, and I've stepped in it. Do you have a paper towel I can use to wipe my sole?"

"Yes, of course." Louise edged her way to the counter and passed the roll, but not without stepping into more of the spill herself.

"Is everyone ready to go?" Ethel asked, coming toward them from the foyer.

"Watch where you walk," Florence warned. "They've had an accident."

Ethel peeked into the room and cried out with dismay. "That bowl has been in the family for ages. I think it was a wedding present when your father and mother married."

That did nothing to make Jane feel better, but she was in emergency mode. Louise hurried off to get a pail of water and a mop. Florence tried to retrieve pieces of the bowl without stepping in the eggs, but she wasn't very successful. Ethel wrung her hands and reminisced about her brother's wedding.

"Is everyone ready to walk?" Clay came to the kitchen door and immediately sized up the problem. "It looks like we have some cleanup to do. Mrs. Buckley, Mrs. Simpson, maybe you ladies should start your walk without me. I'll help clean this up."

"We're really not in a hurry," Ethel said.

"Maybe we shouldn't go at all," Florence said with a little laugh. "It is Friday the thirteenth."

"I didn't think of that." Ethel frowned and seemed to be seriously considering the risk.

Louise came with the mop and water, and Clay took it from her as though it were his responsibility.

"You go enjoy your walk too, Ms. Louise. The cleanup will go faster if there aren't a lot of people in the kitchen."

Louise protested but she might as well have whistled into the wind. Clay wouldn't hear of her helping.

Jane went into the dining room to provide coffee, taking the coffee cake with her as the opening course.

"We've had a kitchen mishap. I'm terribly sorry, but I'll get the rest of breakfast to you as soon as possible."

When Jane returned to the kitchen, Clay had finished the floor and was washing smears from the cupboards.

"I can't believe I'm letting you do this," Jane said gratefully. "You should be sitting at the table with the other guests."

"It's my choice," he said with a winning grin.

She made up a second breakfast for her guests in record time, and soon they were enjoying their main course.

"How can I thank you for all you've done?" Jane asked as Clay helped her put things away and clean up the kitchen.

"I see you still have some coffee cake left. Maybe you could cut me a modest slice."

"Gladly!"

She added her two leftover eggs to his breakfast, scrambling them with cheese and mushrooms, then sat at the kitchen table with him to have a cup of tea and a sliver of the cake. It occurred to her that she still didn't know his plans. Would he be there this evening? She really should ask him, but she didn't have the heart to do it after all the help he'd given her.

The phone rang, and she answered it with a slight foreboding, considering that the day had been pretty much a disaster so far. It was one of the elderly sisters who had booked two rooms for the evening.

"I'm terribly sorry," the younger of the two said on the phone. "We were so looking forward to staying at your inn, but my sister is ill. I took her to the emergency room last night, and there's no way she'll be able to travel today. The doctors are keeping her for observation because she's had heart problems in the past."

Jane expressed sympathy. The double cancellation was bad news. However, there would be a place for Clay if he wanted it.

"There's been an accident! There's been an accident!" Ethel cried out from the foyer, her voice high-pitched and sounding near hysteria.

Jane hurried to meet her, Clay close on her heels.

"What happened?" She didn't see Louise or Florence, which scared her even more than Ethel's incoherent words.

"Slow down, Aunt Ethel. I can't understand what you're saying. Is someone hurt?"

"Of course, someone is hurt. That's what I'm trying to tell you."

"Is Louise all right?"

"I'm fine," her sister said, coming in the front door with Florence's arm draped across her shoulders.

"I tripped in a pothole," Florence said, obviously wanting to tell her own story. "What a disgrace that the town hasn't repaved Berry Lane! God bless Fred Humbert for driving us back here."

"Come sit down," Jane said, leading the way to the kitchen. "Where are you hurt?"

"These slacks won't be good for anything but the rag bag," Florence lamented, sticking out her legs to show Jane the tear over one knee and the dirt stains on both. "Oh, Clay, I'm sure this wouldn't have happened if you'd been with us. We never should have gone walking on Friday the thirteenth. Viola and Carlene both had the good sense to cancel."

"Don't be silly. They didn't cancel for that reason," Louise said, standing in the doorway with folded arms.

"I'm not so sure," Ethel said. "Maybe Carlene did have to go to Potterston to meet with an advertiser, but Viola's excuse didn't sound very convincing to me."

"One of her cats isn't eating," Louise pointed out. "This was the only time she had free to take it to the vet. He was doing her a favor by opening his office early just to see her cat."

"Well, perhaps," Florence said, "but I knew no good would come of going out on Friday the thirteenth."

"Are you hurt?" Jane asked, wondering if she needed to get the first-aid kit.

"She's not bleeding. I checked," Louise said. "But I imagine her knees will be very sore."

"Yes, they will be. I'll have to call Ronald to come get me. You understand about Friday the thirteenth, don't you, Clay? It's in the Bible."

He looked uncomfortable but didn't hesitate to answer.

"Some people think it goes back to the Last Supper," he said thoughtfully.

"Yes, Judas was the thirteenth person, and he betrayed Jesus," Florence responded eagerly.

"But the early Christians didn't believe in that superstition," Clay said in a kindly voice. "Think about it. Jesus ate with his twelve disciples many times. He called them the twelve, and He was the thirteenth. That doesn't suggest that he saw the number as unlucky. And it certainly doesn't say so in the Bible."

"Everyone knows it's an unlucky day," Florence insisted.

"I read a book about the Knights Templar, a group that started during the crusades," Ethel said. "A French king had many members of their religious order arrested on Friday the thirteenth because he owed them a lot of money and wanted more from them. That's how the superstition started."

"Maybe," Clay said, "but in any case, there have always been superstitions. Most date back to pagan religions and shouldn't have any importance to us today."

"But look what a bad day it's been so far. Jane never spills things, and her floor was a disaster when I came here to walk," Florence insisted.

"I was in a hurry. I was careless," Jane admitted. "But wasn't I lucky to have Clay here to help me?"

Perhaps the unlucky cancellations had their good side too. It would have been worse for the two elderly sisters if one had gotten sick away from home. And it also meant Clay could keep the room.

"Your good luck was my bad luck," Florence grumbled.

"Tell you what," Jane said. "There's no reason to call Ronald. I'll drive you home. You probably should elevate your knees and ice them as soon as possible."

"I can drive her—if you don't mind my using your car, Ms. Jane," Clay offered.

"That would be nice of you," Jane agreed. "I do have to go to Potterston this afternoon for groceries, though."

"Maybe I could hitch a ride with you."

"Of course. Now let me help you out to the car, Florence."

"Yes, the sooner I get home, the better. Say what you will, Friday the thirteenth hasn't been a lucky day for me."

Alice finished her shift at the hospital, but she didn't feel that her day's work was done. Today it wasn't Grace Chapel Inn that needed her attention. Instead she absolutely had to decide how to write the article about Maud. None of Carlene's advice was proving helpful, and Alice suspected that it was because she was too close to her subject. Maybe she'd known Maud too long to be objective. Or, more likely, she cared so much about her that she didn't want to fail her. The elderly woman had opened her heart to Alice, and she didn't want the article to sound trivial or contrived.

Still, she had to balance a very moving statement of faith with the guidelines for the newsletter. The wellness committee wanted practical advice on how to stay healthy, but from Alice's viewpoint, physical, mental and spiritual health went hand in hand. She couldn't think of anything that contributed more to all three than a close personal relationship with the Lord.

Her car interior was as hot as it had been the day before, and again she stood outside with the doors open to let the faint breeze cool it a bit. Somewhat to her surprise, she saw a lanky young man with a cowboy hat walking across the parking lot.

"Miss Alice," Clay called out. "You haven't seen Jody, have you?"

"Not today." She looked for Jane's car but didn't see it.

"Ms. Jane dropped me off. She had to do her grocery shopping. I hope I haven't missed Jody."

"You haven't. There's her car," Alice said pointing down the row of parked cars to one that she'd passed.

He grinned.

"Have you had a good day?" Alice asked.

"Not entirely. I didn't go walking with the ladies. Ms. Jane had an accident with a bowl of eggs, and I stayed to help her clean up. Unfortunately Mrs. Simpson tripped in a pothole during their exercise, and that was the end of the walk. She blamed it on Friday the thirteenth, but I tried to talk her out of that."

"One of our patients nearly refused to have emergency heart surgery when he realized what date it was," Alice said. "Fortunately his wife and the physician were persuasive enough to have him go through with it."

"He was fortunate that the Lord gave him sensible people to look after him," Clay said thoughtfully.

"I think you're right," she said.

They were standing on overheated asphalt next to an automobile that was hot enough to hurt her hand if she touched the metal. It was an unlikely place to have this conversation, but she wondered whether Clay could help with her dilemma about the article.

"Clay, perhaps you could help me. I interviewed a woman of ninety-seven about the reasons for her longevity," she began, then went on to explain what had been said.

"She sounds like a wonderful example of faith," he said.

"What I don't know is how to capture it in an article that still meets the requirements of the wellness newsletter. What can I possibly say to convey the depth of her faith?"

"Why, nothing," he said.

"Nothing?" She'd hoped for some inkling of a viable idea from him.

"She's already said it herself." He looked toward Jody's car and smiled broadly. "I have to go now."

He was gone, running toward the young nurse so she wouldn't leave without him. Alice watched for a moment, then felt that she was intruding on their meeting. She got into her hot car, opting to use the air-conditioning for a few minutes to make it bearable.

"She's already said it herself," Alice repeated out loud as she exited the lot.

All the way home she pondered what Clay had said with growing excitement. Maud had spoken from her deepest conviction. Alice didn't need to explain or interpret what she'd said. It was all recorded, ready to be used. There was nothing in the newsletter guidelines that prohibited her from using a direct testimonial.

She rolled down her window and turned off the air conditioner, hardly noticing the hot air that rushed into the car. She had her answer. All she needed to write was a brief introduction. Maud's own words couldn't be improved on and didn't need to be explained.

Usually the Howard sisters had much to talk about at the end of a busy day, but their dinner had been a quiet one. They didn't start sharing thoughts about their daily activities until all three of them were relaxing on the front porch, their feet up and their conversation muted. Jane treasured these quiet times at dusk, and this evening the western sky was a glorious light show with shades of orange and pink that no artist could duplicate.

"I went over to check on Florence," Jane said. "One knee is bruised, but she seems okay otherwise. Ronald is such a sweetheart. He went over to inspect the pothole himself, then got the mayor to promise it would be filled in as soon as the city employees come to work Monday. Not only that, he apparently never suggested that his wife should watch where she's walking."

"There are times when advice is exceedingly unwelcome," Louise said with a smile.

"And times when it's extremely helpful," Alice said. "I was at my wit's end trying to figure out how to write my article about Maud. Clay made everything clear. All I need to do is let her tell her own story in her own words. The solution was right in front of me, but I couldn't see it."

"That young man is a marvel," Jane said. "He's helped me so much that I feel guilty charging him for the room. You wouldn't object if I give him a special discount, would you? I know he has inherited money, but I don't think he's rich. In fact, I get the impression that his walk will use up just about everything he has."

Both sisters murmured agreement. Louise yawned, and Jane felt her eyes drooping shut.

"You know," Alice said, "I'm so sleepy I could drift off right here."

"Wouldn't that be a sight if all three of us slept through the night on the porch?" Jane asked with a soft laugh.

"Alice and I did it sometimes when we were little and our rooms were really hot," Louise reminisced. "You loved it, Alice, but you worried that you'd never get to sleep."

"I did, though. Acorn Hill is really quiet after the sun goes down."

"And every other time," Jane teased.

"I think the guests are all in for the evening," Louise said. "I really should make the effort to go to bed."

"So should I, but I love sitting out here with the two of you," Alice said. "I don't think Clay is back, though. Maybe we should turn on the porch light for him."

"Or we could sit here dozing until he shows up," Jane said with a smile. "I'm too limp and relaxed to move."

"He might think we're keeping tabs on him," Alice pointed out. "I, for one, am headed for bed even though I have the weekend off. This is my catch-up-on-sleep time."

She stood but didn't get as far as the door when a car pulled up in front of the inn. Alice walked to the railing but didn't immediately recognize the vehicle. When two people got out, their voices were unmistakable. Jody had driven Clay back to Grace Chapel Inn.

Apparently they didn't see the sisters in the dark shadows of the porch, so Alice said a loud good evening to make them aware that they weren't alone.

"Oh, is that you, Alice?" Jody called out. "I just gave Clay a ride home. He's leaving tomorrow, you know."

Alice didn't know, but the news was hardly unexpected. He'd stayed far longer in Acorn Hill than he'd planned.

"We'll miss you, Clay," Jane said, speaking for all of them. "You will be here for breakfast, won't you?"

"I wouldn't dream of passing up the best food east of the Mississippi."

If anyone else had said that, it would have sounded like over-the-top flattery, but since it came from Clay, she couldn't doubt his sincerity.

"Well, good-night, Jody, Clay," Louise said, going through the front door into the inn.

Alice followed her, but Jane paused for a minute, wondering what to do about locking up. Clay took the decision from her.

"If you don't mind, I'll lock the door for you when I go up to bed," he said.

"Thank you, Clay. I'll say good-night too."

Jane went up the stairs to her third-floor room, noticing the soft glow of the low-watt bulbs Clay had installed for her. The more she saw of their muted light, the happier she was with them.

Friday the thirteenth was almost over, and Jane had to admit that the good fortune of being here with her sisters outweighed any lingering notions about bad luck.

Before she closed her eyes to sleep, she thanked the Lord for the multiple blessings she enjoyed every day and for His bringing such a devout and wise young man to their inn. She prayed that the rest of his walk would be fruitful and safe, and that he'd continue to find worthy goals for his generous spirit.

Chapter Fourteen

What time would Clay be leaving today? How much longer would she have to cook for the Snypers? Were they really going to open a bed-and-breakfast to compete with Grace Chapel Inn?

Jane's day began with questions she couldn't answer. Although she'd seen Clay last night, she hadn't wanted to question him while he was with Jody. She felt sure that he had stayed beyond the time when his feet would have allowed him to go, and that Jody was the reason.

No matter when Clay left, she wanted to give him a going-away surprise. Since he was traveling light, the best gift was an edible one. To that end, she'd purchased everything needed for a delicious trail mix.

She set out all the ingredients that would go into it and brought out a large metal mixing bowl, feeling a tinge of regret that she'd broken the pretty stoneware one. There was no trick to making a trail mix. With enough good tidbits, it would provide wonderful snacking for Clay as he walked eastward.

Jane poured a generous amount of dried cherries and raw almonds into the bowl, then added sunflower seeds, a must in her opinion. She liked a lot of fruit, so she poured in dried apricots, golden raisins and banana chips, a sweet crunchy favorite. After gently combining them with a wooden spoon, she added minipretzels and a large helping of granola. After the mix was blended, she spooned it into two separate plastic bags, hoping Clay could fit both into his backpack.

By the time Jane finished, Louise came into the kitchen looking sleepy eyed. She was wearing a blue cotton skirt with a nicely pressed, white short-sleeved cotton blouse and a new pair of sporty shoes she'd just purchased.

"Good morning," Jane said cheerfully, in a happy mood after packing her trail mix. "How do your new shoes feel?"

"As good as need be. It's not as if we're speed walking. If I didn't have to keep pace with Aunt Ethel, I'd gladly go back to walking at my own rate."

"But she loves the activity, doesn't she? She virtually glows after one of your walks."

"I'm not sure it's the exercise that does it," Louise said with a small smile. "She dotes on Clay as if he were her grandson. But if walking makes her happy, it's worth the effort."

"I just finished making trail mix for Clay to take along when he leaves." Jane pointed at the full bags on the counter.

"Is he leaving this morning?"

"He hasn't said. I just wanted to be ready if he does."

"You know, I bought one of those throwaway cameras at the beginning of the summer, but I never got around to using it. The film has a long way to go before it expires. I wonder if Clay would like to carry it with him. He could take a few pictures of things that interest him along the way."

"It's small enough to fit in his backpack and not at all heavy. I think that would be a nice gesture," Jane said.

"I'll go upstairs and get it, then I'll still have time to help you with breakfast before walking."

"No need," Jane assured her. "The table is set for the Snypers. Clay seems to like eating in the kitchen with us, so I'll wait until he comes down."

Before Louise returned, Alice came into the kitchen dressed for her Saturday morning walk with her friend Vera.

"The ladies in the walking club look so smart when they go out that I feel grubby in my threadbare jeans and the T-shirt I got from the Alzheimer's walk last spring," she joked. "Where is everyone?"

"I don't know when the Snypers and Clay want to eat breakfast. I slipped up by not finding out last evening."

"Shall I pour the juice?" Alice asked.

"Maybe it would be just as well to wait."

"I should do something to help."

"You could paint the porch," Jane teased.

Louise returned with the disposable camera.

"I tried one of these at a church picnic last year. It worked surprisingly well," she said.

"Are you going to take pictures of your walking club?" Alice asked.

"No, I thought I'd give it to Clay as a small going-away gift. He might get some interesting shots on the rest of his journey."

"That reminds me! I bought a couple packages of moleskin, intending to give them to him. If he puts it on the tender spots on his feet, it might prevent more blisters. I'll go upstairs and get them."

Alice returned quickly with the moleskin in a bag from the pharmacy and added it to the gifts from her sisters.

"I'll put all of it, the trail mix, camera and your sack, out of sight until he actually tells us he's going," Jane said, opening a cupboard to hide them.

Before she could close the cabinet door, Ethel came into the kitchen. She was wearing well-cut pastel-green slacks in a cotton blend and a pale yellow tunic with white flowers. Jane's first thought was that she looked five years younger this morning, although she wasn't sure exactly what age that would be.

"Goodness, are you planning a trip?" she asked, immediately spotting the gifts.

"No, we just gathered a few things for Clay to take with him when he leaves," Jane explained.

"Is he leaving today?" Ethel didn't manage to hide her disappointment.

"I'm afraid so," Alice said. "Jane is going to put them away until he does go. I'm afraid it will be fairly soon since he seems to be able to walk just fine now."

"Oh dear! I'll be right back," their aunt said, hurrying out of the kitchen.

"Now she probably wants to give him a gift too," Alice said. "It would be a sweet gesture, but I hope she remembers that he can't carry much more weight."

Ethel returned with an ivory-colored envelope in her hand, and a moment later Florence arrived, just in time to hear her friend say, "Put this with the other gifts."

"What are the gifts for?" Florence asked before Jane could tuck the envelope out of sight.

"They're only a few practical things that Clay can use when he resumes his walk," Jane said. "Trail mix, a disposable camera and some moleskin."

"When is he leaving?" Florence asked with alarm.

"We don't know for sure," Alice assured her. "Jane made the trail mix, so we put a few little things with it."

"The trail mix will keep a long time," Jane said.

"Good thing I brought my car to the inn," Florence said. "I'll be right back."

When she returned, she was carrying a pharmacy bag.

"I had this in my car. It's never been opened. Before I decided to quit, I bought a bottle of especially good sunscreen for our walks. I'll be happy to give it to Clay. It's certainly something he'll need."

"Before you decided to quit?" Ethel asked with alarm. "Do you mean you're giving up the walking club?"

It was the first time her friends had ever seen Florence look shame-faced. Now that Jane thought about it, she was wearing dressy navy linen slacks and a silky long-sleeved mauve blouse, not anyone's idea of a walking outfit.

"Ronald insists." She pulled herself up to her full height and stuck out her chin, looking very much the picture of resolve. "He's tired of hearing about my bunion, and tripping in the pothole was the final straw. He's buying an exercise bike I can use at home. I'm determined to use it each and every day. The nice thing is that he's promised to give it a try too. If it works out, we can get exercise even when the weather is rainy or snowy. Or hot, like it's been this month."

"But what about our walking club?" Ethel didn't sound ready to accept her friend's decision.

"It really wasn't working," Florence said a bit forlornly. "Viola is too upset about her sick cat to join us, and Carlene always has a dozen other things she has to do. I suspect that when Clay leaves, no one will want to walk anymore."

"I will," Ethel insisted.

Jane felt sorry for her aunt, but maybe an exercise bike was a better choice for Florence.

"Good morning, everyone."

Clay came into the kitchen with his hair damp from a shower. He was wearing the long-sleeved shirt and bandanna that he'd worn when he arrived, and his backpack was dangling from one hand.

"I wonder if I could fill my water bottles at the sink," he said after giving a personal greeting to each of the women in the kitchen.

"Are you really leaving?" Florence asked, sounding as though she were about to lose her best friend.

"I'm afraid I have to," he said regretfully. "I've made commitments along the way, and I'm seriously behind schedule. Staying at Grace Chapel Inn and getting to know all of you has been great. I appreciate everything all of you have done for me, but I have some important contacts to make. My goal is to convince at least three more towns to build walking trails. If that happens, my walk will have been more than worth it. I have one good prospect in Pennsylvania, a group interested in nature trails. I only need to convince them that it's a project worth supporting."

"I wish Acorn Hill had the resources to build one," Florence said wistfully.

"You have a lovely town and lots of quiet side roads for walking," Clay assured her. "The more urban a locale is, the more people need special walking trails."

"Yes, I suppose that's true." Florence brightened a bit.

"You will stay for breakfast, won't you Clay?" Jane asked, a bit surprised by the depth of the regret she felt.

"Maybe a quick bowl of cereal. I want to get started before the sun is high."

"I have French toast all ready to serve."

"It sounds tempting," he admitted.

"I'll fill your water bottles while you eat," Alice offered.

He glanced at his big, clunky wristwatch. "I have fifteen minutes. I guess that's enough time."

"Do you have to leave at a specific time?" Florence asked. "You're going to be on the road for weeks, maybe months. What difference do a few minutes make?"

"Actually, I'm being picked up. I'm going to resume my walk from Potterston since that's where I stopped for first aid."

"Jane always has plenty of food. You could ask the driver to come in," Florence said, not quite able to conceal her curiosity.

"Sorry, I promised to be outside when she comes. Since I'm going to have breakfast, maybe all of you would join me in a blessing."

He even called Jane from the stove so they could join hands standing around the table.

"Thank you, heavenly Father, for the plenitude of this meal and especially for the wonderful friends who've welcomed me into their lives. Bless them, keep them well and let Your grace flow into their lives."

"And dear Lord, thank You for enriching our lives through your faithful servant, Clay," Alice said.

"Bless him and keep him safe and well on his travels," Louise added.

"And bring him back to see us again before we depart this earth," Ethel said in a soft, sad voice.

"Soon," Florence said. "Amen."

Jane was glad she could hide her emotions by fussing with Clay's breakfast. She couldn't remember when a guest had touched all their hearts so profoundly. When she put his French toast and a small pitcher of heated maple syrup in front of him at the kitchen table, Florence remembered the gifts.

"We all have something for you to take with you," she said proudly.

Jane put the pile of offerings on the table in front of him, and Florence appointed herself to explain what each was as he rather hurriedly ate his breakfast.

When only Ethel's remained, Florence picked it up and started to break the seal on the envelope.

"Let Clay open it," Ethel insisted.

He put down his fork and picked it up, carefully sliding his finger under the flap. When he pulled out a folded bill, he looked at Ethel with a puzzled expression.

"It's a two-dollar bill," she said. "My husband used to save money by buying one or two every time he went to the bank. You don't see them now, of course, but in the early 1950s he accumulated enough in an old World War II ammunition box to buy a new Buick for cash. It was so unusual it was in the newspaper. He always carried one in his billfold. He said he'd never be broke if he never took it out."

"This was the one he carried?" Clay sounded as touched as Jane felt.

"Yes, the very same one. I know you don't hold with good luck superstitions and such, but I wanted you to take it with you on the rest of your walk."

"But your children—your grandchildren?"

"How would I choose which one should have it?"

Clay stood up and took Ethel in his arms, giving her a light kiss on her forehead.

"Thank you, Ethel. I'll never forget your generosity."

He thanked each of the women in turn, then packed his gifts into his crowded yellow backpack. Jane went to check him out, not mentioning that she was deeply discounting the amount charged on his credit card. He'd blessed their lives far too much for her to require more thanks. He didn't even look at the receipt she handed him.

With a final wave he ran toward a car that pulled up in front of the inn.

Jane returned to the kitchen, only then remembering that she still had to feed the Snypers. She peeked into the dining room, where they were helping themselves to the coffee she'd left warming on the buffet. They were obviously ready to eat, so she had to hustle.

"You don't have to walk with me. I know I'm too slow for you," Ethel was saying.

"I enjoy your company," Louise assured her.

"I think I'll leave now," Florence said. "I'm so glad that I got to see Clay one more time. I don't suppose we'll ever see him again, but he is such a lovely boy. Do you think it will be in the *Nutshell* when he gets to New York?"

No one had an answer, so she headed toward the front door, seeming more subdued than usual.

"I'm going to think about getting one of those bikes for myself," Ethel said, not sounding very happy about the prospect. "I suppose I could listen to music while I peddled. Or maybe use it in front of the television, although there isn't a whole lot I want to watch. I did think the walking club was Florence's best idea ever. Who would have guessed that she would be the one to quit?"

"Bunions are quite painful," Alice said.

"I can understand Ronald's getting upset about her fall," Jane said. "Florence is resilient, but she could have broken something."

"She wouldn't have fallen if she hadn't been talking a mile a minute while she walked," Ethel complained.

"Tell you what, Aunt Ethel, let's walk while it's still relatively cool outside. Maybe we can talk more about the best way for you to get regular exercise. I love walking around Acorn Hill at any pace, especially in your company," Louise said.

Ethel was persuaded to go walking with her niece, and Alice headed toward the front door with them on her way to meet Vera. She usually met her friend at Fred's Hardware, a convenient place for both of them. Jane shooed both her aunt and her sisters out of the inn. She could easily serve breakfast to the Snypers without her sisters' help.

She was going to poke her head into the dining room to tell them their meal was coming, but she heard rather angry words coming from them. She stopped short, not intending to eavesdrop but not wanting them to see her pass by on the way to the kitchen.

"I still think you should offer ten thousand less," Isabel said. "Think of all the expenses we'll have before we can even start."

"I've thought of all that," Vern insisted. "The seller has already come down. We can't stay here forever. I want this settled. We'll need to hire an architect and get bids."

"You're the one who keeps delaying," his wife said.

Jane quickly slipped past the door, unseen by the Snypers. She'd heard more than she wanted. Apparently they were all ready to purchase the property for their own bed-and-breakfast.

Even though she'd known for some time that it was a possibility, Jane reeled from the news. How could two bed-and-breakfasts survive in a town as small as Acorn Hill? It had been a risk to open one. This could be the end of their business, and Jane couldn't imagine being as happy any place else.

Would they have to sell their father's house? Where would Alice and Louise live if they did? Where would she ever find a chef's job that could compare to being her own boss in a place she loved?

Jane felt like weeping, but there was still breakfast to serve. She put French toast on two plates and added strips of crisp bacon. Determined not to let the Snypers know that she'd overheard them, she moved into the dining room with her manner composed. All seemed quiet after their flare-up, and she hurried to put their plates in front of them, not even pausing to ask if they needed anything else.

Alone in the kitchen, she prayed hard for the strength to deal with whatever was in store for the inn and for her. The unfairness of it was the most difficult to accept. Grace Chapel Inn was more than a business. It was a beacon of hospitality that helped define the small-town values of Acorn Hill.

"No," Jane said out loud to herself.

This was no time to lose faith. If the Lord wanted her to move on to other endeavors, He would give her the courage to do so. She often felt that her sisters' commitment to the Lord was greater than her own. Maybe this was a time of testing. But until the Snypers actually forced their inn to close, Jane resolved not to lose hope.

Chapter Fifteen

*N*o guests at all?"

Louise sat down at the kitchen table for a cup of tea after her walk.

"None," Jane said. "Not tonight or tomorrow night. I can't remember when we've had a whole weekend with all four rooms empty."

"You're certain that the Snypers are leaving today?"

"Yes, they've stayed the length of their reservation. They did ask to leave their things in the room until this afternoon. The really bad news is that I overheard them talking about the place they want to buy. They're making an offer today. We could have real competition once they get their bed-and-breakfast built."

"Oh dear." Louise raised one eyebrow, a sure sign that she was distressed. "That could mean hard times for Grace Chapel Inn, but I'm not going to give up hope this soon. There must be some way to stay competitive."

"I suppose we could have a price war," Jane said glumly, "but we already try to keep guests' costs to a minimum."

"What's going on?" Alice asked, coming into the room.

Her face was pink and moist from her walk, obviously a vigorous one.

"Jane heard the Snypers talking about an offer on the place they want for their bed-and-breakfast," Louise said. "We're trying to think of ways to stay competitive."

"They won't have Jane's wonderful cooking," Alice said.

"There's no reason to believe the Snypers won't serve good breakfasts, but guests do like our Victorian ambiance," Jane said. "Maybe we could do more advertising and emphasize the historic architecture."

"Too bad George Washington never slept here." Alice helped herself to some lemonade from the fridge and joined her sisters at the table.

"What we need is a ghost," Jane joked. "Then we could get on TV."

Louise raised her eyebrow again. "That would be dandy, the inn overrun by ghost-hunters."

"It would be a bit bizarre." Jane pursed her lips thoughtfully. "I'm just trying to think of a selling point if we have to compete with a brand-new bed-and-breakfast."

"Our selling point has always been hospitality. Guests who come here from larger cities are enchanted by our small town and the peaceful atmosphere," Alice reminded them.

"You're right, of course," Jane agreed. "We can't be something we're not, but I can't help being concerned about dwindling income."

"We all are," Louise assured her, "but we can't panic over a bad patch. Sometimes we have to turn away people who want to stay. And we have quite a number of regulars who make return visits."

"Think of this weekend as a minivacation," Alice suggested. "There are worse things than having the house to ourselves for a couple of days."

"One bit of good news," Louise said. "I think I've convinced Aunt Ethel that she doesn't need a walking club to keep fit. She's seriously considering a stationary bike for herself. I've promised to take her to Potterston so she can see the different options. It's possible she might even buy a treadmill."

"That's wonderful," Jane said. "I know the group walked too slowly for you, but something good has come of it."

"Now if Jody writes the wellness articles for me, the weekend won't be a total loss," Alice said. "I've made arrangements for one of the women on the hospital staff to type up the interview with Maud. It will be a big relief when the newsletter is ready to be printed."

"Maybe I'll look in on her this afternoon," Jane said. "I enjoy our visits as much or more than she does."

"Her appetite isn't good. Maybe you can take something to tempt her," Alice suggested.

"I have a container of chicken noodle soup in the freezer that I can take along. If it is a typical visit, I'll return refreshed by her faith and spirit."

Outside, the pavement sizzled under a relentlessly hot sun, but the house was a tranquil haven, the lower floor naturally cool with all the windows wide open. Alice was enjoying the peace and quiet. Both of her sisters were out and about, Jane making her call on Maud, and Louise shopping with Ethel. One of them needed to stay behind to check out the Snypers, and Alice had been glad to do it.

She was running a dust mop around the foyer when she heard a rather timid knock on the front door. Guests and townspeople knew that it was all right to walk in, so Alice hurried to answer it.

"Jody, how nice to see you," she said, surprised because she hadn't expected her to bring the completed articles this soon.

"I hope I'm not disturbing anything," she said.

Alice noticed that her young friend was looking better all the time. Today she was wearing pink and white seersucker shorts with a white cotton knit tank top, a simple outfit but one that showed off her shapely legs and the creamy skin of her arms. But it wasn't clothing that had transformed the shy young woman. She had a glow that could only be attributed to happiness, puzzling because she had been so upset about Clay's departure.

"Let's go into the kitchen," Alice said. "I think there's a pitcher of freshly squeezed lemonade in the fridge. I can't think of anything that tastes better on a hot day like this."

As soon as she was seated, Jody took a folded paper out of her oversize canvas purse and laid it on the table.

"I'm afraid I haven't finished both articles, but I did start the diabetes interview. I wanted you to see it to be sure I'm on the right track."

"I'll be happy to read it, but you didn't need to drive all the way here."

Alice was a bit puzzled because there was only a single page, short enough to have read over the phone. She scanned it quickly and was very pleased. Jody got right to the point, and she also wrote in a way that made the reader want to keep going.

"It's really very good," she said.

"Thank you." Jody flushed with pleasure. "It wasn't the writing that made me change my mind about being a journalist, you know. But I'm glad I did. It's much more satisfying being able to help people as a nurse. Clay says—"

She broke off as though she wasn't sure whether she wanted to share what he'd said.

"My sisters and I were so sorry to see him go," Alice said, wanting to give Jody a chance to say what she'd come to say. It obviously wasn't solely about the article, which had a very smooth, professional start.

"I'm sorry I bothered you with my worries," Jody slowly began. "I should have had more faith that things would work out."

Have they worked out? Alice wondered. *Is it possible Clay hasn't left? But that wouldn't make sense considering his dedication to his cause—and it's unlikely that Jody would be here if he is still in Potterston.*

"You didn't bother me. I'm always happy to hear anything you want to say," Alice assured her.

"Yes, you're a wonderful friend. That's why I wanted you to know how much Clay and I have come to mean to each other. I know, we've hardly had a chance to get to know each other well. My mother says nothing will come of it because he'll be gone so long. But sometimes it isn't about time. We both know we're meant to be together."

Alice shared at least a little of her mother's doubt. How long would it take Clay to reach his destination? Weeks? Months? She was a little apprehensive about the young couple's chances after a long separation, but her own experience told her that it was possible. Certainly her love for Mark Graves never completely died, and recently it had been renewed on a deeper, more spiritual level than would have been possible before he came to accept the Lord as his Savior. The fact that their jobs still kept them apart in no way affected the way they felt about each other.

"Clay's a lovely person." Alice could say this with complete sincerity.

"I love him, Alice. I never thought it could happen to me, but he's changed my whole life. I've never met anyone like him."

"Does he have plans . . . for when the walk is finished?" She didn't want to dampen Jody's enthusiasm, but she really did wonder what the future held for him.

"He's thought a lot about going to a seminary. That's part of what his walk is about, time to really think through what he wants to do with the rest of his life. If he feels that the Lord has called him, that's what he'll do."

"From the little time I've known him, I think he would make a wonderful minister."

Alice still wondered how Jody could fit into a long-term commitment to the Lord. Since her own mother had died young, Alice had been her father's companion and helpmate, sometimes a demanding job given the needs of even a small congregation like Grace Chapel.

"What I really want to tell you," Jody said, "is that Clay is coming back. As soon as he finishes his walk, he's going to get here in the fastest possible way—plane, train or auto. If he decides to fly, I'll meet him at the airport."

"That's so nice." It was all Alice could think to say.

"It's wonderful! We'll talk about our future plans then, but neither of us doubts that we'll be together. It was meant to be, a gift from the Lord that we even met. What if he hadn't gotten blisters? What if you hadn't invited me to your cookout? It makes me tremble to think that we might have gone on with our separate lives, never knowing that we missed the one person in the world destined to be a soul mate."

"He's an exceptionally loving person. The women here were so pleased that he walked with them in the mornings. Just by being with them, he convinced my aunt and her friend that they needed to give wellness a priority in their lives."

"He has that gift. He doesn't need to lecture or preach to people. His life is an inspiration. Oh, Alice, I'm so happy I feel like shouting to the whole world that I love Perry Clay Garfield."

"You know, I believe you do," Alice said with a heartfelt smile.

"I'm taking up too much of your time, but I just had to tell someone who would understand."

"I'm sure your mother will realize how serious you are, especially after Clay returns. She just doesn't want you to get hurt."

"I guess you're right. I'll just have to give her time to accept it. Unfortunately, my father hasn't been home the whole time Clay was here, but I have a feeling that he'll approve as soon as he meets him."

"There's no reason why he shouldn't. I hope when Clay comes back, the two of you will come here to see us."

"You'll be the first to hear our good news," Jody promised. "Clay couldn't say enough wonderful things about the way you and your sisters welcomed him. He's never stayed in a place where he felt so much at home so quickly. He loved the little gifts all of you gave him, but I'm afraid he wasted all the film on me."

"Hardly a waste." Alice smiled.

"He didn't have a picture of himself to give me, but he said one will be in the next issue of the Acorn Hill newspaper. Do you think I could get a copy of that issue?"

"I'll ask the editor for the photo."

"Thank you, thank you, thank you." Jody jumped up and hugged Alice.

"I'd better go now," the younger woman said. "Clay promised to call when he found a place to stop for the night, not that it's anywhere near late enough now, but I have some errands to do. I'll get right at the articles when I get home. I promise you won't be disappointed."

"I'm sure I won't. I'm really happy things are working out so well for both of you."

"Thank you so much for all you've done. Bye now." Jody hugged her again and hurried out the front door.

Alice couldn't stop smiling long after Jody left. Her happiness had been the perfect tonic to drive away worries about Grace Chapel Inn's future. Jody had so much faith in Clay's promise to return that Alice scolded herself for ever wavering in her belief that, with the Lord's help, things would work out well for them.

Jane always felt buoyed by a visit with Maud, and today was no exception. The elderly woman never complained about the aches and pains of advanced age, and she was so positive in her attitude that Jane never failed to come away in a sunny mood.

If more people took the time to visit the aged and infirm, their own lives would be greatly enriched, she thought.

When she got back to the inn, Alice was still excited about Jody's news. The two of them temporarily forgot about the dark cloud hanging over Grace Chapel Inn in their delight for the young couple.

"I think I'll run to the pharmacy for a few things now that you're back," Alice said. "The Snypers haven't come to claim their luggage and check out yet."

"I'll watch for them. Oh, and thanks for suggesting that I take something. Maud was happy to have the soup."

Jane went into the kitchen to plan an evening meal. She could create a big salad to serve with fresh rolls. She'd found some especially mild onions yesterday along with alfalfa sprouts and an avocado. For extra crunch she could add thin slices of cucumber to the romaine lettuce and cherry tomatoes she had on hand.

Instead of beginning the preparations, she sat at the kitchen table thinking about everything that had happened that week. At least she could never complain that life was dull running a bed-and-breakfast.

Jane was startled from her ruminations when the front door slammed loudly. A moment later she heard the Snypers heatedly discussing something. She gave them a few minutes to get up to their room before she went out to the registration desk.

They came down loaded with luggage and still discussing something about property.

"Oh, Jane, we'll be leaving now," Vern said.

"I hope you enjoyed your stay," Jane said, repeating what she said to all departing guests.

"It was a colossal waste of time," he said.

"Not that we didn't enjoy your hospitality," Isabel said apologetically. "It's just that things didn't work out quite the way we'd hoped."

"We wouldn't have hung around here so long if that real estate agent had been up front with us sooner," Vern grumbled. "Can you imagine, we nearly made a binding offer on a site next to property that an oil company has optioned? Fine bed-and-breakfast that would be with a view of a gas station."

Isabel looked uncomfortable. She avoided looking directly at Jane.

"I'm inclined to believe that the agent didn't know until now. She wasn't involved with the oil company," his wife said.

"*Humph!*"

"You know, Jane," she said, "it's been my retirement dream to have a bed-and-breakfast of my own, but maybe this is a blessing in disguise. I've seen how hard the three of you work to make this place special. The more we learned about what's involved, the more doubts I've had."

"I wish you would have told me that a week ago," her husband said, sounding more resigned than angry. "I have a business to run in the here-and-now."

"You probably wondered why we asked so many questions," Isabel said. "I'm sorry if we pried into your business too much."

"It's a small town," Jane said. "We did have an inkling that you were interested in starting a bed-and-breakfast of your own."

"And you were still so gracious to us! What wonderful people you are!" Isabel exclaimed. "Even if I never have a bed-and-breakfast of my own, I won't forget the lovely experience we've had here and the Christian kindness that you and your sisters have shown."

"Good breakfasts," Vern somewhat grudgingly admitted. "Hard on the waistline though."

He patted his midsection.

"No one made you take seconds and thirds," his wife teased, sounding more relaxed now that she'd admitted the reason for their stay.

"Well, good luck to you," her husband said. "If everything is settled, we'll be off now. Oh, by the way, there's a small tear in the shower curtain. You might want to check that out."

"Thank you, I'll do that."

Jane couldn't suppress a smile as they went out the front door, both of them loaded to capacity with luggage. She couldn't wait to tell her sisters that there wouldn't be a second bed-and-breakfast in Acorn Hill, but she did feel a twinge of conscience for her unexpressed hostility toward the couple.

Dear Lord, she silently prayed, *give me the grace to react with charity and Christian love if I'm ever faced with a situation like this again. Forgive me my unkind thoughts and negative feelings. And thank You for my loving sisters. Their example is a beacon on my spiritual journey. In the name of Lord Jesus. Amen.*

Alice returned first. When she heard the good news, she grabbed Jane and did a little dance around the kitchen.

Louise came into the kitchen a few minutes later, pleased that Ethel had decided to consider buying a treadmill.

"She thought the exercise bike might be too much for her. If she does get a treadmill, she can exercise whenever she likes, and the weather won't be a problem."

"Our day has certainly taken a turn for the better," Alice said. "Jane has good news too."

"The Snypers decided not to buy the property for a bed-and-breakfast. There's a possibility that a service station will be built right next to the land they wanted."

Louise's reaction was more restrained than Alice's but no less happy.

"What a relief! I've been crunching numbers in my head since I first heard that we might have competition. I don't believe our small town has enough visitors to keep two bed-and-breakfasts in business."

"We still have an empty inn for the weekend," Jane reminded them. "Maybe we should worry that Acorn Hill can't support one."

"I don't believe that," Alice said optimistically. "Not for one minute."

The phone rang, and Jane went out to the reservations desk to answer it so she could hear over her sisters' happy conversation. It was several minutes before she came back to the kitchen.

"You look like a cat who's been lapping cream," Alice said.

"Tell us why you're grinning from ear to ear," Louise insisted. "Has something good happened?"

"That was Maud Schoonamaker's daughter. The family has good news to celebrate. Maud's great-granddaughter just got engaged. They want Maud to meet her fiancé, so they planned a spur-of-the-moment reunion here in Acorn Hill. Maud's house is so tiny that there's no way all of them can stay there. In fact, her daughter is worried that any overnight guest would tax her strength too much. They badly need rooms tonight and tomorrow night. Her daughter called from Potterston, wondering if there was any chance we had a room or two vacant so they wouldn't all have to stay in a motel there."

"I thought you just visited Maud," Louise said. "Did she say anything about her family's coming?"

"They didn't tell her ahead of time because they knew she would try to clean and cook for them."

"How many rooms?" Louise asked.

"Four! Can you believe we have a full house for the weekend? I think a breakfast casserole might be best. Her daughter asked if they could bring Maud for breakfast, so I'll have to think about something to tempt her appetite. I wonder about popovers. They're easier than they look."

"That's our Jane," Alice said laughing.

"It seems our business is booming again," Louise agreed.

"Neither of you ever lost faith," Jane said, hugging both of them before she rushed to the fridge to start planning.

About the Authors

*P*am Hanson and Barbara Andrews are a daughter-mother writing team. They began working together in the early 1990s and have had twenty books published, including fifteen under the pseudonym Jennifer Drew.

Pam has taught reporting courses at West Virginia University and is now director of advising for the School of Journalism. She has presented writing workshops and has been involved in school and church activities. She lives with her husband, a professor, and their two sons in West Virginia, where she shares her home with her mother.

Previous to their partnership, Barbara had twenty-one novels published under her own name. She began her career writing Sunday-school stories and contributing to antiques publications. Currently she writes a column and articles about collectible postcards. For more than twenty years she has sponsored a mail postcard sale with all proceeds going to world hunger relief. She is the mother of four and the grandmother of seven.

Tales from Grace Chapel Inn

Back Home Again
by Melody Carlson

Recipes & Wooden Spoons
by Judy Baer

Hidden History
by Melody Carlson

Ready to Wed
by Melody Carlson

The Price of Fame
by Carolyne Aarsen

We Have This Moment
by Diann Hunt

The Way We Were
by Judy Baer

The Spirit of the Season
by Dana Corbit

The Start of Something Big
by Sunni Jeffers

Spring Is in the Air
by Jane Orcutt

Home for the Holidays
by Rebecca Kelly

Eyes on the Prize
by Sunni Jeffers

Summer Breezes
by Jane Orcutt

Tempest in a Teapot
by Judy Baer

Mystery at the Inn
by Carolyne Aarsen

Saints Among Us
by Anne Marie Rodgers

Never Give Up
by Pam Hanson & Barbara Andrews

Once you visit the charming village of Acorn Hill, you'll never want to leave. Here, the three Howard sisters reunite after their father's death and turn the family home into a bed-and-breakfast. They rekindle old memories, rediscover the bonds of sisterhood, revel in the blessings of friendship and meet many fascinating guests along the way.